HOMETOWN HEARTS

Mother in Training

USA TODAY Bestselling Author

MARIE FERRARELLA

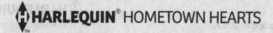

HARLEQUIN® HOMETOWN HEARTS

Recycling programs
for this product may
not exist in your area.

ISBN-13: 978-0-373-21485-3

Mother in Training

Printed in U.S.A.

HOMETOWN HEARTS

SHIPMENT 1

Stranger in Town by Brenda Novak
Baby's First Homecoming by Cathy McDavid
Her Surprise Hero by Abby Gaines
A Mother's Homecoming by Tanya Michaels
A Firefighter in the Family by Trish Milburn
Tempted by a Texan by Mindy Neff

SHIPMENT 2

It Takes a Family by Victoria Pade
The Sheriff of Heartbreak County by Kathleen Creighton
A Hometown Boy by Janice Kay Johnson
The Renegade Cowboy Returns by Tina Leonard
Unexpected Bride by Lisa Childs
Accidental Hero by Loralee Lillibridge

SHIPMENT 3

An Unlikely Mommy by Tanya Michaels
Single Dad Sheriff by Lisa Childs
In Protective Custody by Beth Cornelison
Cowboy to the Rescue by Trish Milburn
The Ranch She Left Behind by Kathleen O'Brien
Most Wanted Woman by Maggie Price
A Weaver Wedding by Allison Leigh

SHIPMENT 4

A Better Man by Emilie Rose
Daddy Protector by Jacqueline Diamond
The Road to Bayou Bridge by Liz Talley
Fully Engaged by Catherine Mann
The Cowboy's Secret Son by Trish Milburn
A Husband's Watch by Karen Templeton

SHIPMENT 5

His Best Friend's Baby by Molly O'Keefe
Caleb's Bride by Wendy Warren
Her Sister's Secret Life by Pamela Toth
Lori's Little Secret by Christine Rimmer
High-Stakes Bride by Fiona Brand
Hometown Honey by Kara Lennox

SHIPMENT 6

Reining in the Rancher by Karen Templeton
A Man to Rely On by Cindi Myers
Your Ranch or Mine? by Cindy Kirk
Mother in Training by Marie Ferrarella
A Baby for the Bachelor by Victoria Pade
The One She Left Behind by Kristi Gold
Her Son's Hero by Vicki Essex

SHIPMENT 7

Once and Again by Brenda Harlen
Her Sister's Fiancé by Teresa Hill
Family at Stake by Molly O'Keefe
Adding Up to Marriage by Karen Templeton
Bachelor Dad by Roxann Delaney
It's That Time of Year by Christine Wenger

SHIPMENT 8

The Rancher's Christmas Princess by Christine Rimmer
Their Baby Miracle by Lillian Darcy
Mad About Max by Penny McCusker
No Ordinary Joe by Michelle Celmer
The Soldier's Baby Bargain by Beth Kery
The Maverick's Christmas Baby by Victoria Pade

To Patience Smith, the kind keeper of my sanity.

Thank You

Chapter One

January

The short, squat man moved his considerable bulk between her and the front door, blocking her line of vision. The look on his round, florid face fairly shouted of exasperation.

"You know how a watched pot don't boil?" he asked her. "Well, a watched door don't open, neither. So stop watching the door and start doing somethin' to earn the money I'm paying you, Zoo-ie."

Zooey Finnegan grimaced inside. Milo Hanes, the owner of the small Upstate New York coffee shop where she currently clocked in each morning in order to draw a paycheck, seemed to take an inordinate amount of pleasure mispronouncing her name.

Most likely, she thought cynically, it was a holdover from his days as the schoolyard bully.

That was okay, she consoled herself. It wasn't as if waitressing at the coffee shop was her life's ambition. She was just passing through. Just as she'd passed through a handful of other jobs, trying them on for size, searching for something that would arouse a passion within her, or at least awaken some heretofore dormant potential.

Her parents had been certain that her life's passion would be the family furniture business. As the firstborn, she'd been groomed for that ever since she was old enough to clutch a briefcase. They and her uncle Andrew had sent her off to college to get a business degree, and after that, an MBA.

The only problem was, Zooey had no desire to acquire a degree—not in business, at any rate.

Her family had made their money designing and selling stylish, affordable furniture. What had once been a small, single-store operation had branched out over the years to include several outlets, both in state and out. Proud as she was of their accomplishments, Zooey couldn't picture herself as a company executive, or a buyer for the firm, or even a salesperson in one of their seven showrooms. As far as she was concerned, Finnegan's Fine Furniture was going to have to remain fine without her.

She loved her parents, but she refused to be browbeaten by them into living a life of not-so-quiet desperation. Stating as much had led to "discussions," which led to arguments that indirectly resulted in her breaking up with Connor Taylor. Her parents felt he was the perfect man for her, being two years older and dedicated to business. What he was perfect for, it turned out, was the company. He'd upbraided Zooey when she'd told him her plans, saying she was crazy to walk away from such a future.

That was when she'd realized Connor was in their relationship strictly for the money, not out of any all-consuming love for her. If it had been the latter, she'd informed him, he would have been willing to hike into the forests of Oregon and subsist on berries and grubs with her. Declaring that she wanted to be mistress of her own destiny, she'd had a huge fight with everyone involved—her parents, her uncle and Connor. When her parents threatened to cut off her funds, she'd done them one better. She'd cut them off and left to find her own way in the world.

So far, her "way" had led her to take up dog walking, to endure a very short stint as a courier, and now waitressing. None of the above proved to be very satisfying or fulfilling. As a dog walker, she'd managed to lose one of her charges. As a courier she'd gotten lost three times in two days, and her first week's pay as a waitress went to repay Milo for several cups and saucers she'd broken when she'd accidentally tilted her tray.

A lesser woman might have given up and gone home, but Zooey had her pride—and very little else. Cut off from the family and the family money, she was running out of options as well as cash. The rent on her closet-like apartment was due soon, and as of right now, she was still more than a hundred dollars short.

She supposed she should have been worried, but she wasn't. Zooey was, first and foremost, a die-hard, almost terminal, optimist. She refused to be beaten down by circumstances, or a scowling boss who could have doubled as a troll in one of *Grimm's Fairy Tales.*

Something would come along, she promised herself. After all, she just didn't have the complexion to be a homeless person.

In the meantime, she still had a job, she reminded herself.

Offering Milo a spasmodic smile, she went back to mechanically filling the sugar containers on each of the small tables and booths scattered throughout the coffee shop. As she worked, Zooey tried not to look toward the door. Or at least, not to appear as if she was looking toward the door.

He was late.

Rubbing away a sticky spot on the table with the damp towel she had hanging from her belt, Zooey couldn't help wondering if anything was wrong.

Jack Lever, the drop-dead-gorgeous blond criminal lawyer who came in every morning for coffee and a blueberry muffin—and secretly lit her fire—hadn't turned up yet. It wasn't like him.

She'd met Jack her first day on the job. He'd been sitting at her station, with an expression that indicated he had the weight of the world on his shoulders. Being of the opinion that everyone could use a little friendly chatter and, at times, a shoulder to lean on, she'd struck up a conversation with him.

Or, more accurately, a monologue. She'd talked and he'd listened. Or appeared to. After about a week of relative silence on his part, Jack finally offered more than single-word responses to her questions.

Given something to work with, she let her questions grow lengthier and progressively more personal than just inquiries about how he liked the weather, the Mets, his muffin. Week number two had actually seen the beginnings of a smile on his lips. That was when her heart had fluttered for the first time. That was also when she'd almost spilled coffee on his lap instead of into his cup.

She began to look forward to Jack's daily stops at the shop. A couple of times, he put in more than one appearance, dropping by around lunchtime the two days he was in the area because of a case. The county courthouse was only two blocks away.

He was a creature of habit as much as she was a free spirit. And he always, always came into the shop around the same time. Eight thirty. It was almost nine now.

"Maybe Mr. Big Shot's cheating on you

with another coffee shop," Milo said, chuckling into his two chins as he changed the industrial-size filter for the large steel coffee urn. Steam hissed, sending up a cloud of vapor as he removed the old filter.

Milo had caught her looking again, she realized, averting her eyes from the door and back to the sugar container in her hand. Zooey shrugged, her thin shoulders moving beneath the stiff, scratchy white cotton uniform. It chafed her neck a little.

She saw no point in pretending she didn't know what her boss was talking about. "Maybe he took a vacation day."

"Or maybe his wife did," Milo commented.

Zooey was about to tell the man that Jack was a widower. It was the latest bit of personal information he'd shared with her. Eighteen months ago, his wife had been killed in a hit-and-run car accident, leaving him with two small children to raise: a girl, Emily, who was about seven now, and a little boy, Jack Jr., still in diapers. The boy was almost two.

But the information never reached her lips. Milo was nodding toward the door.

Zooey turned around in time to see Jack Lever walking in. He was herding a little girl before him, while holding tightly on to a boy who looked as if he was ready to explode in three different directions at once. Jack was also trying to hang on to his briefcase.

Zooey's heart went out to him immediately. The man was obviously struggling, and while she would have bet even money that Jack Lever was a formidable opponent on the courtroom floor, he looked as if he was in over his head at the moment.

Kids did that to you, she thought. She had a younger brother who'd been a pistol when he was around Jack Jr.'s age.

Abandoning the sugar dispenser, Zooey made her way over to Jack and his lively crew. She flashed her brightest smile at him, the one her father had once said could melt the frown off Satan.

"Hi. Table for three?" she asked, her glance sweeping over the two children before returning to Jack.

"More like a cage for two," he murmured wearily under his breath.

Zooey's eyes met his. He would have looked more refreshed wrestling alligators. "Tough morning?"

He gazed at her as if he thought she had a gift for severe understatement. "You might say that." Jackie tried to dart under a table, but Jack held fast, pulling him back. "My nanny quit."

"You don't have a nanny, Daddy." Emily giggled shyly, covering her small, pink mouth with both hands.

The sigh that escaped his lips measured 5.1 on the Richter scale. "And as of seven this morning, neither do you."

Zooey deliberately led the three to a booth, feeling that the enclosed space might make it easier for Jack to restrict the movements of his children. Just before she turned to indicate that they should take a seat, she grabbed hold of two booster seats stacked in the corner and slid one on each side of the table. Then, because Jack seemed to be having more trouble with the boy, she took him by the waist and lifted him in the air.

"Up you go, young man."

Because she added a little bounce to the descent, Jack Jr. laughed gleefully, his eyes lighting up. He clapped his hands together. "Again," he cried.

Zooey winked at him, leaning over to make sure that he was securely seated. "Maybe when you leave."

The little girl was tugging on the short

apron Zooey wore. When she looked at her quizzically, Emily said shyly, "You're pretty."

Straightening, Zooey beamed. "Well, thank you, honey."

The smile on Emily's lips faded just a little as sadness set in. "My mommy was pretty, too," she added quietly.

Poor baby, Zooey couldn't help thinking. She deliberately avoided looking at Jack, feeling that the moment had to be awkward for him.

"She would have had to have been," Zooey told her, running a hand over the girl's vivid blond hair. "Because you are."

Jack saw his daughter all but sparkle in response.

It suddenly hit him. For the first time since they'd opened their eyes this morning, his children were quiet. Both of them. At the same time.

Stunned, he looked at the young woman he'd been exchanging conversation with for the last six weeks, seeing her in a brand-new light. That of a sorceress. "How did you do that?"

Looking up from the children, Zooey smiled at him beatifically. "Do what?"

"Get them to quiet down like that. They've

been making noise nonstop all morning." Even Emily, whom he could usually count on to behave herself in his company, had been more than a handful today. When it rained...

The waitress's green eyes were smiling as she looked at the two children again. "Maybe they're just worn-out," she suggested modestly.

The truth of it was she had a way with kids. She always had, having gotten her training early in life while learning to keep her brothers and sisters in line. The fact that it had resembled more of a conga line than anything drawn using a straight edge was the secret of her success.

Zooey raised her eyes to Jack's. He was, after all, the customer. And undoubtedly running late. "The usual?" she asked.

It took him a second to get his mind in gear. And then he nodded. "Yes, sure."

Emily cocked her head, trying to understand. "What's the usual, Daddy?"

"Coffee and a blueberry muffin," Zooey answered before he had the chance. The little girl made a face. Zooey laughed. "How does hot chocolate with marshmallows bobbing up and down sound to you?"

The grimace vanished instantly, replaced by a wide grin. "Good!" Emily enthused.

"Messy," Jack countered.

"The nice thing about messy," Zooey told him, giving the towel hooked on her belt a tug, "is it can always be cleaned up." And then she looked from one child to the other. "But you guys aren't going to be messy, are you?"

Emily shook her head solemnly from side to side. Watching her, Jack Jr. imitated the movement.

Zooey nodded, trying hard to match the children's solemnity. "I didn't think so. By the way, my name's Zooey." She held her hand out to Emily.

The little girl stared at it, stunned, before finally putting her own hand into it. "Emily," she said with the kind of pride and awe a child felt when she suddenly realized she was being treated like an adult.

"Jackie," the little boy announced loudly, sticking his hand out as if he was gleefully poking a snake with a stick.

Zooey shook the little boy's hand and never let on that the simple gesture made her own hand sticky. Without missing a beat, she took her towel and wiped off his fingers.

"Pleased to meet you, Jackie. You, too, Emily. I'll be right back with your hot chocolates," she promised, backing away. "And the usual," she added, looking at Jack before she turned on her heel to hurry to the kitchen.

Jack leaned back in the booth, blowing out a long breath. Trying to get his bearings. And focus.

He didn't often believe in miracles. Actually, he didn't believe in them at all. They weren't real and, contrary to popular belief, they just didn't happen. Miracles belonged in legends, something for the desperate to cling to in times of strife.

And then he smiled to himself at the irony of it. God knew he certainly fit the desperate criteria today. More so than usual.

At exactly five minutes after seven this morning, just as he was preparing to call her to ask why she was running late, the children's latest nanny had called to tell him that she wasn't coming back. Ever. And then she'd hung up.

He could only assume that the soured old woman had spent the night mulling over this declaration of abandonment, brought on by the disagreement they'd had yesterday evening regarding her strict treatment of the children. Emily had tearfully told him she'd been punished that morning because she'd accidentally spilled her glass of milk at the table. Since there wasn't a single truly willful bone in the little girl's petite body, he knew Emily hadn't done it on purpose.

But apparently Agnes Phillips did not tolerate anything less than perfection. This wasn't the first time she and Jack had locked horns over her uptight behavior. He'd taken her to task on at least two other occasions. And she'd only been in his employ a little over two months.

Obviously, the third time was *not* the charm, he thought cynically. He'd been planning on replacing the woman as soon as he could get around to it. Agnes had undoubtedly sensed it and, reject from a military camp though she was, had beaten him to the punch by calling up and quitting.

Leaving him in a hell of a bind.

He felt like a man in the middle of the ocean, trying to survive by clinging to a life raft that had just sprung a leak.

Jack had a case due in court today and he didn't think that Alice, the receptionist at his law firm, was going to be overly thrilled about his need to turn her into a babysitter for a few hours.

But observing the way both his children seemed to light up the moment the young waitress returned with their hot chocolates gave him food for thought.

"Zooey?"

She placed his coffee and muffin down on the table and very carefully pushed the plate before him. She raised her eyes to his, wishing she could clear her throat, hoping she wouldn't sound as if something had just fluttered around her navel at the sound of his deep voice saying her name. "Hmm?"

He leaned forward across the table, his eyes never leaving hers. "I'd like to offer you a bribe."

"Excuse me?" Zooey withdrew the tray from its resting spot on the table and held it to her like a bulletproof shield that could protect her from everything, including handsome lawyers with drop-dead-gorgeous brown eyes.

"Maybe I'd better backtrack."

"Maybe," she agreed firmly.

He slanted a glance at his children. Jackie was already wearing a hot chocolate mustache on his cheeks. "Look, I told you their nanny quit this morning."

Out of the corner of her eye, Zooey saw several other customers come through the door and take seats. She knew that she should be easing away from Jack, turning a deaf ear to his problems. But the kids looked as if they were about to drive him over the edge.

Jack delivered the final, hopefully winning, salvo. "And I'm due in court today."

More customers came in. Zooey caught the eye of Debi, the other waitress, mouthing, "Can you get those tables?"

"And there's no room for short assistants?" she asked out loud, turning back toward Jack.

He didn't crack a smile at her comment. "None."

Zooey paused, thinking. But it was a foregone conclusion as to what she'd come up with: nothing. "I'd like to help you out," she told him apologetically, "but I don't know of anybody who could watch them."

He hadn't wanted a substitute. "I was thinking of you."

"Me?" She glanced toward Milo. He was behind the counter, pretending not to listen. She knew better. The man had ears like a bat on steroids. "I've already got a job. Such as it is," she couldn't help adding.

Her lack of enthusiasm about her job was

all the encouragement Jack needed. "I'll pay you double whatever he's giving you."

That still didn't amount to all that much, she thought. But this really wasn't about money. It was about time. "Double? I don't th—"

"Okay." He cut in, not letting her finish. "Triple. I'm a desperate man, Zooey."

And gorgeous. Don't forget gorgeous, she added silently. And triple her pay would go a long way toward helping her with her bills.

Jack could see that he had her. All he needed was to reel her in. "It'd only be for the day," he assured her. "You could take them to the park, the mall, wherever—"

Something suddenly hit her. She put her hand up to stop him before he could get any further.

"Mr. Lever. Jack. You're talking about leaving your kids with me. Your *children*," she emphasized. "And you don't even know me." What kind of a father did that make him—besides desperate?

He knew all he really needed to know about the young woman, he thought. It wasn't as if she had kept to herself. She'd been open and forthright even when all he'd wanted with his coffee and muffin was a side order of silence.

"We've talked for six weeks." He picked another point at random. "And I know you like jazz. And," he added, his voice growing in authority, "you're conscientious enough to point out that I don't know you."

A smile crept over her lips, even as she stooped to pick up the spoon Jackie had dropped. "Isn't that like a catch-22?"

Jack nodded. "And you're intelligent," he added, then played his ace. "And I'm desperate."

Zooey couldn't help the laugh that rose to her lips. "Intelligent and Desperate. Sounds like a law firm in an Abbott and Costello routine."

Jack looked mildly surprised. He didn't expect a twenty-something woman to be even remotely familiar with the comedy duo from the forties and fifties. "Anyone who knows things like that is above reproach," he told her.

He didn't need to flatter her, Zooey thought. The man had her at "hello."

"Okay, if I'm going to do this, I'm going to need some information," she told him, mentally rolling up her sleeves. "Like where you work, where you live, how to reach you in case of an emergency, where and when to meet you so that you can take your children home...."

She was thorough; he liked that. She was asking all the right questions, questions he would have given her the answers to even if they'd been unspoken. "I knew I wasn't wrong about you."

"The day is young," she deadpanned. Then, because she'd never been able to keep a straight face for long, she grinned. "Just give me a few minutes to clear it with my boss."

Jack was aware of every second ticking by as he automatically glanced at his watch.

"I'll make it fast," she promised, already backing away from the table.

"I like her, Daddy," Emily told him in a stage whisper that would have carried to the last row in Carnegie Hall.

"Lucky for us, she feels the same way," he told his daughter.

Zooey returned to their table faster than he'd anticipated. Jack rose to his feet, scanning her face. Looking for an unspoken apology. To his relief, there was none.

"All set," she announced.

He glanced toward the counter. The man behind it was scowling and sending him what could only be referred to as a dark look. "Your boss is all right with this?"

"He's fine with this," she replied. Jack noticed she was carrying her jacket and that she was now slipping it on. "He doesn't care what I do."

Jack raised an eyebrow. And then it hit him. "He fired you."

Zooey shrugged dismissively. She wasn't going to miss the itchy uniform. "Something like that."

Jack hadn't meant for this to happen. "Look, I'm sorry. Let me talk to him."

But Zooey shook her head. "You're running late, and besides, I was thinking of leaving soon, anyway. This is just a little sooner than I'd originally planned," she admitted. And then she smiled down at the two eager faces turned to her. The children had been following every word, trying to understand what was going on. "You two ready to have fun?"

Chapter Two

The last word Jack Lever would use to describe himself was *impulsive*.

It just wasn't his nature.

He was thorough, deliberate and didactic. Born to be a lawyer, he always found himself examining a thing from all sides before taking any action on it.

It was one of the traits, he knew, that used to drive his wife, Patricia, crazy. She'd complain about his "stodgy" nature, saying she wanted them to be spontaneous. But he had always demurred, saying that he'd seen too many unforeseen consequences of random, impetuous actions to ever fall prey to that himself.

It was, he thought, just one of the many stalemates they'd found themselves facing. Stalemates that had brought them to the brink of divorce just before she was killed.

However, he thought as he slipped case notes into his briefcase, this was an emergency. Emergencies called for drastic measures. Tomorrow was going to be here before he knew it. Tomorrow with no nanny, with Emily needing to be dressed and taken to school, and Jackie still a perpetual challenge to one and all.

Walking out into the hall, Jack made his way to the elevator and pushed the down button. He needed a sitter, a nanny. A person with extreme patience and endless fortitude.

The express elevator arrived and he got on, stepping to the rear.

Desperate though he was, it seemed that fate—the same fate that had sent him three ultimately unsatisfactory nannies, one worse than the other—had decided to finally toss him a bone.

Or, in this case, a supernanny.

So when he stepped out of the fifteen-story building where the firm of Wasserman, Kendall, Lake & Lever was housed, and saw Zooey sitting on the stone rim of the fountain before the building, one child on either side of her and none looking damaged or even the worse for wear, Jack decided to go with his instincts. And for once in his life, do something impulsive.

The moment she saw Jack exiting the building, Zooey rose to her feet.

"Daddy's here," she told the children. A fresh burst of energy sent Jackie and Emily running madly toward their father.

Jackie reached him first, wrapping his small arms around his father's leg as high as they would reach. "Hi, Daddy!" he crowed. For a little boy, he was capable of a great deal of volume.

"Hi, Daddy." Emily's greeting was quieter, but enthusiastic nonetheless.

He'd dropped his briefcase to the ground half a beat before Jackie and Emily surrounded him. "Hi, yourselves," he said, wrapping an arm around each child.

Jack did like being a father. He just had no idea how to exercise small-person control.

Finding himself in a large conference room with a collection of the state's greater legal minds, or in a tiny briefing area with a known hardened criminal, Jack knew how to handle himself. Knew how to maintain control so that the situation never threatened to get away from him.

But when it came to dealing with the under-fifteen set, especially with small beings who barely came up to his belt buckle, he was at a complete loss as to what to do.

Not so Zooey, he thought. Being with the children seemed to be right up her alley. As a matter of fact, she appeared to be as fresh as she always was when he walked into the coffee shop each morning.

He had no idea how she did it. His children had worn out three nannies in the last eighteen months, and seemed destined to wear out more.

Unless his instincts were right.

Slipping his arms free, he nodded at the short duo. "Did they give you any trouble?" he asked, almost afraid of the answer.

Zooey looked at him, wide-eyed. "Trouble? No!" she replied with feeling.

The way her green eyes sparkled as she voiced the denial told Jack that today had not been a boring one by any means.

Though he didn't spend all that much time with them, he knew his kids, knew what they were capable of once they were up and running.

"Should I be writing out a check to anyone for damages they or their property sustained?"

She grinned. "You really do sound like a lawyer. No, no checks. No damages. Emily and Jackie were both very good."

He stared at her. The trip to the parking structure that faced his office building and presently contained his car was temporarily aborted. "You sure you're talking about my kids?"

She laughed, and it was a deep, full-volume one. "I am sure," she assured him. "We went to the park, then saw that new movie, *Ponies on Parade,* had a quick, late lunch and here we are."

Ponies on Parade. He vaguely remembered promising Emily to take her to that one. He guessed he was off the hook now. And damn grateful for it. He looked at Zooey with awe and respect. "You make it sound easy."

"It was, for the most part."

Zooey thought it best to leave out the part that while she was taking Emily to the ladies' room, with Jackie in tow, the latter had gotten loose and scooted out from under the stall door. He'd managed, in the time it had taken her to leave Emily and go after him, to stuff up a toilet with an entire roll of toilet paper he'd tossed in and flushed.

Moving fast, Zooey had barely managed to snatch him away before the overflowing water had reached him.

Jack had always been very good at picking up nuances. He studied her now. "Something I should know about?"

The man had enough to deal with in his life, Zooey thought. He didn't need someone "telling" on Jackie. "Only that they're great kids."

"Great kids," Jack echoed, ready to bet his bottom dollar that that wasn't what had been on her mind at all.

But, when he came right down to it, he knew Emily and Jackie were that. Great kids.

They were also Mischievous with a capital *M*. Kids who somehow managed to get into more trouble than he could remember getting into throughout his entire childhood.

Reflecting back, Jack had to admit that he'd been a solemn youngster—an only child whose father had died when he was very young. For years, Jack had thought that it had somehow been his fault, that if he'd been a better person, a better son, his father would have lived.

His stepfather did nothing to repair the hole that doubt had burrowed into his soul. He was never around during Jack's childhood. He'd been, and still was, a terminal workaholic, laboring to provide a more than comfortable lifestyle for Jack's mother, a woman who absolutely worshipped money and everything it could buy. Growing up, Jack supposed it could be said that he'd had the best childhood money could buy.

Everything but attention and the sense that he was truly loved.

He studied Zooey's expression now. "You mean that?"

"Of course I do." Why would he think anything else? she wondered. "I wouldn't say it if I didn't mean it." Truth was something she had the utmost respect for. Because once lost, it couldn't be easily won back. Like with Connor, she thought, then dismissed it. No point in wasting time there.

About to grasp Jackie's hand to help lead him across the street to the parking structure, Zooey saw that the little boy had both arms raised to her, a silent indication that he wanted to be carried. She scooped him up without missing a beat.

Holding him to her, she glanced toward

Jack. "Nothing worse than lying as far as I'm concerned." She would have expected that, as a lawyer, he should feel the same way. But then, she'd always been rather altruistic and naive when it came to having faith in people, she reminded herself.

Holding Emily's hand, Jack waited beside Zooey for the light to turn green. He read between the lines. "Somebody lie to you, Zooey?"

Connor, when he said he loved me, and all the while he was in love with the family business. And the family money. She wasn't about to share that with Jack no matter how cute his kids were.

Instead, she shrugged her shoulders. "No one worth mentioning."

The slight movement reminded her that the uniform she had on still chafed. She hadn't had a chance to go home and change before taking on the task of entertaining Jack's children.

One movement led to another, and it was all she could do to keep from scratching. "I guess I'd better get out of this uniform and give it back to Milo."

The light turned green and they hurried across the street.

Reaching the other side, Jack glanced at her. "So, you really are fired?"

Zooey nodded.

In his estimation, she didn't look too distressed about it. Which he couldn't begin to fathom. From what she'd told him, he knew that Zooey lived by herself and didn't have much in the way of funds to fall back on. If it had been him, he would have been sweating bullets. But then, if it had been him, he wouldn't have been in that position to begin with.

Jack was nothing if not pragmatic. "What are you going to do for money?"

"I guess I'm going to have to hunt around for another job." She looked up at him brightly, tongue-in-cheek. "Know someone who wants to hire a go-getter who makes up in enthusiasm what she lacks in experience?"

He surprised her by answering seriously. "As a matter of fact, I do."

Zooey had asked the question as a joke, but now that he'd answered her so positively, she was suddenly eager. This meant no hassles, no scanning newspapers and the Internet. No going from store to store in hopes that they were hiring.

It was nice to have things simple for a change.

"Who?"

And this was where Jack allowed himself to be impulsive. "Me."

The parking garage elevator arrived and they got on. Zooey stared at him, dumbfounded. "You?"

He nodded, wondering if she was going to turn him down, after all. Until this moment, he hadn't considered that option.

"I need a nanny." He heard Emily giggling again. "The kids need a nanny," he corrected. "And you need a job. Seeing as how you got fired doing me a favor, the least I can do is hire you." He paused, then added the required coda. "If you want the job." The last thing he wanted was for her to feel that he was trying to railroad her, or pressure her into agreeing. He might be desperate, but she had to *want* to do this.

Zooey narrowed her eyes, trying to absorb what he was saying. He'd always struck her as being a cautious man, someone who believed in belts *and* suspenders. Normally, she found that a turnoff. But there was something about Jack Lever, not to mention his looks, that negated all that.

"You'll pay me to watch your kids?"

"It's a little more complex than that, but yes."

Zooey looked at him guilelessly. "Sure."

He really hadn't expected such a quick response from her. All the women he'd previously interviewed for the job had told him they would have to think about it when he made an offer. And they'd wanted to know what benefits would be coming to them. Zooey seemed to be the last word in spontaneity. Patricia would have loved her.

"You don't want to think about it?"

Zooey waved her hand dismissively. "Thinking only clutters things up." And then she hesitated slightly. "One thing, though."

Conditions. She was going to cite conditions, he thought. Jack braced himself. "Yes?"

A slight flush entered her cheeks. She looked at him uncomfortably. "Could you give me an advance on my salary?" He gazed at her quizzically, compelling her to explain the reason behind the request. "I sort of owe a couple of months back rent and the landlord is threatening me with eviction."

From out of nowhere, another impulsive thought came to Jack. He supposed that once the gates were unlocked, it seemed easier for the next idea to make its way through.

He refrained from asking her the important question outright, preferring to build up to it. "Do you like where you live?"

The elevator had reached the fourth level. Zooey got out behind Jack and Emily. A sea of cars were parked here.

Like was the wrong word, she thought, reflecting on his question. She didn't like the apartment, she made do with it. Because she had to.

"It's all I can afford right now," she admitted. "More than I can afford," she corrected, thinking of the amount she was in arrears. A whimsical smile played on her lips as she added, "But that'll change."

Did she have a plan, or was that just one of those optimistic, throwaway lines he knew even now she was prone to? "It can change right now if you'd like."

Zooey's smile faded just a tad as she looked at him. A tiny bit of wariness appeared. She was not a suspicious person by nature—far from it. For the most part, she was willing to take things at face value and roll with the punches.

But she was also not reckless, no matter what her father had accused her of that last day when they'd had their big argument, just before she'd taken her things and walked out, severing family ties as cavalierly as if they were fashioned out of paper ribbons.

"How?" she asked now.

"You can move in with me. With us," Jack quickly corrected, in case she was getting the wrong idea. "As a nanny." He moved Emily forward to underscore his meaning. "There's a guest room downstairs with its own bath and sitting area. From what you mentioned, it's larger than your apartment."

She rolled his words over in her head. It wasn't that she minded jumping into things. She just minded jumping into the *wrong* things.

But this didn't have that feel to it.

Zooey inclined her head. "That way I could be on call twenty-four/seven."

"Yes." And then he realized that might be the deal breaker. "No." He shook his head. "I didn't mean—"

Zooey couldn't help the grin that rose to her lips. Here he was, a high-priced criminal lawyer, actually tripping over his tongue. Probably a whole new experience for him.

He looked rather sweet when he was flustered, she thought.

She was quick to put him out of his misery.

"That's all right, Jack. I don't mind being on call twenty-four/seven. That makes me more like part of the family instead of the hired help."

Jack wasn't all that sure he wanted to convey that kind of message to Zooey. Right now, he had all the family he could handle. More, really, he thought, glancing at the deceptively peaceful-looking boy she held in her arms.

But as Jack opened his mouth to correct the mistaken impression, something cautioned him not to say anything that might put her off. He was, after all, in a rather desperate situation, and he wanted this young woman—the woman his children had taken to like catnip—to accept the job he was offering her. At least temporarily.

If things wound up not working out, at the very least he was buying himself some time to find another suitable candidate for the job. And if things *did* work out, well, so much the better. There was little he hated more than having to sit there, interviewing a parade of nannies and trying to ascertain whether or not they were dependable. So far, every one he'd hired had turned out to be all wrong for his children. Neither Emily nor Jackie *ever* liked who he wound up picking.

This was the first time they had approved.

And he had a gut feeling about Zooey. He had no idea why, but he did. She was the right one for the job.

Emily was becoming impatient, tugging on his hand. He pretended not to notice. His attention was focused on Zooey. "So does that mean you'll take the job?"

She wasn't attempting to play coy, she just wanted him to know the facts. "Seems like neither one of us has much choice in the matter right now, Jack. You've got your back against the wall and so do I."

She smiled down at Emily. The little girl seemed to be hanging on every word. In a way, Emily reminded Zooey of herself at that age. As the oldest, she'd been privy to her parents' adult world in a way none of her siblings ever had. There was no doubt in her mind that Emily understood what was going on to a far greater extent than her father thought she did.

Zooey winked at the little girl before looking up at Jack. "Lucky for both of us I enjoy kids."

As a rule, Jack liked having all his *i*'s dotted and his *t*'s crossed. She still hadn't actually given him an answer. "Then you'll take the job?"

He was a little anal, she thought. But that was all right. As a father, he was entitled to be, she supposed. "Yes, I'll take it." And then she looked at him, a whimsical smile playing on her lips. "By the way, how much does the job pay?"

She was being cavalier, he thought. Her attitude about money might have been why she'd found herself in financial straits to begin with. He was annoyed with himself for not having told her the amount right up front. He told her now, then added, "According to the last nanny, that's not nearly enough."

Zooey did a quick calculation in her head, coming up with the per-hour salary. She had always had a gift for math, which was why her father had been so certain that getting an MBA was what she was meant to do. Zooey liked numbers, but had no desire to do anything with them. The love affair ended right where it began, at the starting gate.

Jack was going to be paying her more than twice what she'd gotten at her highest-paying job so far. She wondered if that was the going rate, or just a sign of his desperation.

"That should have been your first clue," she told him glibly.

He didn't quite follow her. "Clue?"

"That the woman was all wrong for the job." Still holding the sleeping Jackie, she ran a hand over Emily's hair. Zooey was rewarded with sheer love shining in the girl's eyes. "Nobody takes this kind of job to get rich," she informed him, "even at the rates you're paying. They do it because they love kids. Or at least, they should."

Reaching his car, Jack dug into his pocket for his keys. Once he had unlocked the vehicle, Zooey placed the sleeping boy in his arms.

This time, Jackie began to wake up, much to his father's distress. The ride to his Upstate New York home wasn't long, but a fussing child could make it seem endless.

"You're leaving?" Even as he asked her, he was hoping she'd say no.

But she nodded. When she saw the distress intensify, she told him, "Well, I do have to get my things from my place."

But Jack wasn't willing to give up so easily. "Why don't you come home with us tonight, and then I'll help you officially move out on the weekend?"

Zooey raised her auburn eyebrows and grinned. "What's the matter, Jack, afraid I won't come back?"

"No," he told her adamantly. And then, remembering her comment about the truth, admitted, "Well, maybe just a little." Once the words were out, he was surprised by his own admission. "You know, what with time to think and all."

"You don't have anything to worry about," she assured him. "This is the best offer I've had since I left college."

He noticed that she'd said "left" rather than "graduated." He wondered if lack of funds had been responsible for her not getting a degree. If she worked out, he might be tempted to help her complete her education, he decided. That would definitely get her to remain.

"Give me your home address, Jack. And your home phone number," Zooey added. "Just in case I get lost." Her eyelid fluttered in a quick wink. "I'll be at your house bright and early tomorrow morning, I promise. By the way, when is bright and early for you?"

"Six-thirty."

"Ouch." At that hour, she'd be more early than bright, she thought. "Okay, six-thirty it is."

Setting Jackie in his car seat, Jack wrote out his address and number. Reluctantly.

Wondering, as he gave her the piece of paper and a check for the advance she'd asked for earlier, if he was ever going to see her again.

Chapter Three

October

Zooey could still remember, months later and
comfortably absorbed into the general routine of the Lever household, the expression
of relief on Jack's handsome face that first
morning she'd arrived on his doorstep. She'd
had her most important worldly possessions
stuffed into the small vehicle, laughingly referred to as a car, that was parked at his curb.

Funny how a little bit of hair coloring could
throw a normally observant man for a loop.
When she'd taken the job at the coffee shop,
she'd been at the tail end of her experimen-

tal stage. Auburn had been the last color in a brigade of shades that had included, at one point, pink, and several others that were more likely to be found in a child's crayon box than in a fashion magazine.

Going back to her own natural color had seemed right as she opted to assume the responsibility of caring for a high-powered lawyer's children.

It was the last thing she'd done in her tiny apartment before she turned out the lights for the last time.

It had certainly seemed worth it the next morning as she watched the different expressions take their turn on Jack's chiseled face.

Finally, undoubtedly realizing that he'd just been standing there, he had said, "Zooey?" as if he were only seventy-five percent certain that he recognized her.

She'd drawn out the moment as long as she could, then asked, "Job still available?"

"Zooey," he repeated, this time with relief and conviction. A second later, he moved back, opening the door wider.

She had only to step over the threshold before she heard a chorus of, "Yay! Zooey's here." And then both children, Jackie in a sagging diaper and Emily with only one sock and shoe on, an undone ribbon trailing after her like the tail of a kite, came rushing out to greet her.

Jack had continued staring at her. "Why'd you dye your hair?" he finally asked.

"I didn't," she'd replied, laughing as two sets of arms found her waist, or at least made it to the general vicinity. Neither child seemed the slightest bit confused by the fact that she had golden-blond hair instead of auburn. "I undyed it." Raising her eyes from the circle of love around her, she'd looked at him. "It just seemed like the thing to do, that's all." She couldn't explain it to him any better than that. "This is my natural hair color."

Jack had nodded slowly, thoughtfully, as if the change in color was a serious matter that required consideration before comment.

And then he'd said something unexpected. And very nice. "I like it." It was the first personal comment he had addressed to her.

Hard to believe, she thought now, as she threw on cutoff jeans beneath the football jersey she always wore to bed and slipped her bare feet into sandals, that nearly ten whole months had gone by since then. Ten months in which she'd discovered that each day was a completely new adventure.

She'd also discovered that she liked what she was doing. Not that her life's ambition had suddenly become to be the best nanny ever created since Mary Poppins. But Zooey did like the day-to-day life of being part of a family—a very important part. Of caring for children and seeing to the needs of a man who went through life thinking of himself as the last word in self-sufficiency and independence.

The very thought made Zooey laugh softly under her breath. She had no doubt that Jack Lever was probably hell on wheels in a courtroom, but the man was definitely *not* self-sufficient. That would have taken a great deal more effort on his part than just walking through the door and sinking into a chair. Which was practically all he ever did whenever he did show up at the house.

There were days when he never made it back at all, calling to say that he was pulling an all-nighter. There was a leather sofa in the office that he used for catnaps.

She knew this because the first time he'd called to say that, she'd placed dinner in a picnic basket and driven down to his office with the children. He'd been rendered speechless by her unexpected appearance. She and the kids had stayed long enough for her to put out his dinner, and then left. He was still dumb-struck when she'd closed the door.

Zooey wondered absently if her employer thought the house ran itself, or if he even re-alized that she was not only "the nanny," but had taken on all the duties of housekeeper as well.

It was either that, she thought, or watch the children go hungry, running through a messy house, searching for a clean glass in order to get a drink of water. Taking the initiative, she did the cooking, the cleaning, the shopping and the laundry, when she wasn't busy play-ing with the children.

She was, in effect, a wife and mom—with-out the fringe benefits.

As far as she knew, no other woman was on the receiving end of those fringe benefits. Jack Lever was all about work.

So much so that his children were not get-ting nearly enough of his company.

She'd mentioned that fact to him more than once. The first time, he'd looked at her in sur-prise, as if she'd crossed some invisible line in the sand. It was obvious he wasn't accus-tomed to having his shortcomings pointed out to him, especially by someone whose paychecks he signed. But Zooey was nothing if not honest. There was no way she would have been able to keep working for him if she had to hold her tongue about something as important as Emily and Jackie's emotional well-being.

"Kids need a father," she'd told him outright, pulling no punches after he'd said he wasn't going to be home that night. That made four out of the previous five nights that he'd missed having dinner with Emily and Jackie.

He'd scowled at her. "They need to eat and have a roof over their heads as well."

Men probably trembled when he took that tone with them, Zooey remembered thinking. But she'd stood up to her father, reclaiming her life, and if she could survive that, she reasoned that she could face anything.

"And the food and roof will disappear if you come home one night early enough to read them a story before bedtime?" she'd challenged.

He'd looked as if he would leave at any second. She was mildly surprised that he remained to argue the point. "Listen, I hired you to be their nanny, not my conscience."

She'd gazed at him for a long moment, taking his full measure. Wondering if she'd been mistaken about Jack. Then decided that he was worth fixing. And he needed fixing badly. "Seems like there might be a need for both."

Her nerve caught him off guard. But then, he was becoming increasingly aware that there was a great deal about the woman that kept catching him off guard, not the least of which was that he found himself attracted to her. "If there is, I'll tell you."

"If there is," she countered, "you might not know it. Takes an outsider to see the whole picture," she added before he could protest.

Jack blew out a breath. "You take an awful lot on yourself, Zooey."

In other words, "back off," she thought, amused. "Sorry, it's in my nature. Never do anything by half measures."

He'd made a noise that she couldn't properly break down into any kind of intelligible word, and then left for work.

He'd come home earlier than planned that night. But not the night that followed or any of the nights for the next two weeks.

Still, she continued to hope she'd get through to him, for Emily and Jackie's sake.

Jack was a good man, Zooey knew. And he did love his kids in his own fashion. The problem was, he seemed to think money was a substitute for love, and any kid with a heart knew that it clearly wasn't.

Someone, she thought, heading out of her bedroom toward the kitchen, had given the man a very screwed up sense of values. There was no price tag on a warm hug. That was because it was priceless.

She smelled coffee. Zooey knew for a fact that she hadn't left the coffee machine on last night.

Walking into the kitchen, she was surprised to see that Jack was already there. Not only had he beaten her downstairs, he was dressed for the office and holding a piece of burned toast in one hand, a half glass of orange juice in the other.

Not for the first time, she saw why he'd always come into the shop for coffee and a muffin. The man was the type to burn water. From the smell of it, he'd done something bad to the coffee.

"Good morning," she said cheerfully, crossing to the counter and the struggling coffeemaker. Taking the decanter, she poured out what resembled burned sludge—she'd never seen solid coffee before—and started to clean out the pot. "Sit down," she instructed, "and I'll make you a proper breakfast."

He surprised her by shaking his head as he consumed the rest of the burned offering in his hand, trying not to grimace. "No time. I'm due in early."

She glanced at her wristwatch; this was way ahead of his usual schedule. "How early?"

He didn't bother looking at his own watch. He could *feel* the time. "Half an hour from now." He washed down the inedible toast with the rest of his orange juice and set the glass on the counter. "Traffic being what it is, I should already be on my way."

"Without saying goodbye to the kids?" This was a new all-time low. She thought that pointing it out to him might halt him in his tracks.

Instead, he picked up his briefcase. "Can't be helped."

Zooey abandoned the coffee she was making. "Yes, it can," she insisted. Grabbing a towel, she dried her hands, then tossed the towel on the back of a chair. "I can get them up now." She saw impatience cross his face, and made a stab at trying to get through to him. "They go to sleep without you, they shouldn't have to wake up with you already gone as well."

An exasperated sigh escaped his lips as he told her, "Zooey, I appreciate what you're doing—"

If time was precious, there was none to waste. Zooey cut to the chase. "No, you don't. You think I'm a pain in the butt, and I can live with that. But the kids shouldn't have to be made to live without you. For God's sake, Jack, they see the mailman more than they see you."

He didn't have time for her exaggerations. "I have to leave."

Zooey stunned him by throwing herself in front of the back door, blocking his exit. "Not until you see the kids."

There were a hundred things on his mind, not the least of which was mounting a defense for a client who was being convicted by the media on circumstantial evidence. Jack didn't have time for this.

"This is a little too dramatic, Zooey," he informed her, "even for you."

He'd come to learn very quickly into her stay with them that the young woman he'd hired to watch over his children was not like the nannies who had come before her. Not in any manner, shape or form.

It seemed to him that if Zooey had an opinion about something he'd done or hadn't done, he heard about it. And if he was doing something wrong as far as the children were concerned, he'd hear about that, too. In spades.

While he found her concern about the children's welfare reassuring and their love for her comforting—absolving him of whatever guilt he might have for not taking a more active part in their lives—there were times, such as now, when Zooey went too far.

He glanced at his watch. "Zooey, I'm due in court in a little over an hour."

She stared at him, unfazed. "The longer you argue with me, the more time you lose."

His eyes narrowed as his hand tightened on his briefcase. "I could physically move you out of the way."

Zooey remained exactly where she was. "You could try," she allowed. And then she smiled broadly. "I know moves you couldn't even begin to pronounce."

He knew of her more than just passing interest in martial arts. Late one evening, he'd come across her on the patio as he investigated the source of a series of strange noises he'd heard. He'd found her practicing moves against a phantom assailant, and remembered thinking that he would feel sorry for anyone stupid enough to try anything with her.

Looking at her now, Jack had his doubts that she would use those moves against him. But he wasn't a hundred percent sure that she wouldn't. She was adamant when it came to the children.

He tried to appeal to her common sense. This was way before the usual time when Emily and Jackie got up. "You'll be waking them up."

Zooey appeared unfazed by the argument. "They'll be happy to see you. Besides, they have to get up soon anyway. I've got to get Emily ready for school."

He'd forgotten. The months seemed to swirl by without leaving an impression. It was October already. School had been in session for over four weeks now. There were times he forgot that his daughter went to school at all.

Maybe because he hadn't really become involved in her life, he still tended to think of Emily as a baby, hardly older than Jack Jr.

But even Jackie was growing up.

Jack blew out a breath. "Okay, let's go. I don't have time to argue."

Zooey beamed. She was generous in her victory. "That's what I've been saying all along." Still standing in the doorway, she gestured toward the rear of the house. "After you."

He eyed her, picking up on her meaning immediately. "Don't trust me?"

Growing up around her parents and uncle had taught her the value of diplomacy. Her parents were experts at it. So Zooey smiled, declining to answer his question directly. "Better safe than sorry."

They went to Emily's room first.

The little girl was fast asleep. Fanned out across her pillow, her hair looked like spun gold in the early morning sunbeams. Coming to the side of the bed, Zooey gently placed her hand on Emily's shoulder. She lowered her head until her lips were near her ear. "Emily, honey, your daddy wants to say goodbye."

One moment the little girl was asleep, the next her eyes flew open and she bolted upright.

Her expression as she looked at her father was clearly startled. And frightened. She clutched at his arm as if that was all there was between her and certain oblivion.

"You're leaving, Daddy?"

I knew this was a bad idea, Jack thought darkly. He ran his hand over the silky blond hair. "I've got to go, honey. I've got an early case in court today and Zooey seemed to think you wouldn't be happy unless I said goodbye."

Instantly, the panicky look was gone. The small, perfect features relaxed. She was a little girl again instead of a tiny, worried adult.

"Oh, that kind of goodbye." A smile curved her rosebud mouth. "Okay."

Jack was completely confused. He looked at Emily uncertainly. "What other kind of goodbye is there, honey?"

"Like Mommy's," his daughter told him solemnly.

This time, he raised his eyes to Zooey's face, looking for some sort of explanation that made sense. "What is she talking about?"

Zooey's first words were addressed to Emily, not him. "I'll be back in a few minutes to help you get ready, honey. In the meantime, why don't you lie down again and rest a little more."

"Okay." Emily's voice was already sleepy and she began to drift off again.

Turning toward Jack, Zooey hooked her arm through his. "C'mon," she whispered, as if he'd been the one to wake Emily up, and not her. Tugging, she gently drew him out of the room.

"What's she talking about?" he asked again the moment they cleared the threshold.

Instead of answering, Zooey looked at him for a second, searching for something she didn't find. He didn't know, she realized. But then, he hadn't been there during Emily's nightmares, hadn't seen the concern in the little girl's eyes whenever he was late getting home without calling ahead first.

"Emily is afraid that you're going to die."

Her answer flabbergasted him. He stared at her incredulously.

"What? Why?" he demanded. He hadn't done anything to make Emily feel that way. What had Zooey been telling her?

"Because her mother did," she answered simply, then went on quickly to reassure him in case he thought there was something wrong with Emily. "It's not an uncommon reaction for children when they lose one parent to be clinging to the other, afraid they'll die, too, and leave them orphaned. That's why I wanted her to see you before you left. So she knows that you're fine and that you're coming home to her. She needs that kind of assurance right now."

"So now you're into child psychology?" Jack didn't quite mean that the way it came out. His tone had sounded sarcastic, he realized. But it wasn't in him to apologize, so he just refrained from saying anything.

She treated it as a straightforward question. To take offense would be making this about her, and it wasn't. It was about the children.

"I dabbled in it, yes. Took a couple of courses," she added.

Jack was silent for a moment, then nodded toward his son's room. "And what's Jackie's story?"

"He picks up on Emily's vibrations," Zooey told him frankly. "Except at his age, even though he's very bright, he doesn't know what to make of them." And then she smiled. "Mostly, he just wants his daddy around. Like any other little boy."

Jack had never been one of those fun parents, the kind featured in Saturday morning cartoon show ads. He hadn't the knack for children's games, and his imagination only went as far as drafting briefs. He couldn't see why his children would care about having him around.

"Why," he demanded, "when they have you?"

"I'm more fun," Zooey admitted, "but

you're their daddy and they love you just because of that. It's only natural that they'd want you to be part of their lives," she continued, when he didn't look as if he understood. "And for them to want to be part of yours. An important part," she emphasized, "not just an afterthought."

Jack shook his head. The lawyer in him was ready to offer a rebuttal to what she'd just said. But he held his tongue. Because deep down, part of him knew that Zooey was right. That he should be part of their lives far more than he was.

But right now, it wasn't possible. The demands on his time were too great, and he had to act while he could. That was how careers—lasting, secure careers—were made.

Lucky for his children—and him—he'd struck gold when he'd found Zooey.

He supposed that made a good argument for going along with impulse—as long as it could stand to be thoroughly researched, he added silently. Old dog, new tricks, he mused.

Standing before his son's door, Jack paused for half a second as he looked at Zooey over his shoulder. The harsh expression on his face had softened considerably. "Am I paying you enough?"

"Probably not," she responded, then waved him on. "Now go say goodbye to your son if you don't want to be late."

Now she was looking out for him as well. Jack shook his head. "Anyone ever tell you that you're too bossy?"

The list was endless, she thought, but out loud she said, "Maybe. Once or twice. I wouldn't have to be if you did these things on your own. Now open the door," she told him.

"Yes, ma'am," he murmured, amused, as he turned the doorknob.

Chapter Four

"See, that wasn't so hard, now was it?" Smiling broadly, Zooey shot the question at him three minutes later as she walked with him to the front door.

He stopped in the entry, a less than patient reply on his lips. It froze there as something seemed to crackle between them. It wasn't dry enough to be static electricity, but certainly felt like it.

And like something a little more…

Feeling like a man who was tottering on the brink, Jack pulled himself back. "I didn't say it would be hard, I said that it was—oh, never mind." He waved a hand in the air, dismissing the exchange he knew he'd be destined to lose. "I guess I should just be grateful that you're not with the DA's office."

Her eyes crinkled as she grinned. She was going to get lines there if she wasn't careful, he thought.

"Attaboy, Jack. Always look at the positive side of things."

He didn't believe in optimism. The last time he'd felt a surge of optimism, he'd asked Patricia to marry him—hoping, unrealistically, for a slice of "happily ever after." What he'd wound up getting were arguments and seemingly irreconcilable differences—until her life, and their marriage, was abruptly terminated.

"I deal in facts," he told Zooey tersely.

Was that pity in her eyes? And what was he doing, anyway, staring into her emerald-green eyes.

"Facts can be very cold things," she told him. "At the end of the day, dreams are what get you through, Jack. Hopes and dreams are a reason to get up and strive tomorrow."

Had he *ever* been that idealistic? He sincerely doubted it. If he had, it was far too long ago for him to remember. "Mortgage payments and college tuition are reasons to get up and strive tomorrow."

Zooey cocked her head, her eyes looking straight into him. Into his soul. The touch of her hand on his felt oddly intimate.

"Don't you ever have any fun, Jack?"

He tried to shrug off the feeling undulating through him, the one she seemed to be creating. "You mean I'm not having fun right now?"

The expression on her face told him she took his flippant remark seriously. "You are if you love your work."

"I'm good at it." There was no pride in his answer. It was just another fact.

Zooey shook her head. He could have sworn he detected a whiff of jasmine.

"Not what I said. Or asked." Her eyes seemed to search his face. "Do you love your work, Jack?"

Love was too damn strong a word to apply to something like work, he thought. "When everything comes together, there is a surge of…something, yes."

The answer did not satisfy her.

He was a hard man to pin down, she realized. She wondered if he knew that, or if this verbal jousting was unintentional.

"A 'surge' isn't love, Jack." Zooey's voice softened a little and she leaned forward to smooth down his collar. "Love is looking forward to something. To thinking about it when you don't have to because you want to. Love is anticipation. And sacrifice."

She was standing too close, he thought. *He* was standing too close. But stepping back would seem almost cowardly. So he stood his ground and wondered what the hell was going on. And why. "For a single woman you seem to know a lot about love."

"Don't have to have a ring on your finger to know about love, Jack." The smile on her lips seemed to somehow bring her even closer to him. "Do *you* know about love?"

Okay, now he knew where this was headed. She was trying to get him to spend more time at home. Which would have been fine—if somehow his work could do itself. But it couldn't. "If you're asking me if I love my children, yes, I love my children. I also don't want them doing without things."

Again she moved her head from side to side, her eyes never leaving his. Where did she get off, passing judgment? Telling him how to be a father when she'd never been a parent? The desire to put her in her place was very strong, almost as strong as the desire to take her in his arms and kiss her.

Exercising the extreme control he prided himself on, Jack did neither.

"The first thing they shouldn't be doing without," she told him softly, "is you."

Okay, it was time to bail out. Now. "This conversation is circular."

His harsh tone did not have the desired effect on her. "That's because all roads lead to 'Daddy.'"

Retreat was his only option. So with a shrug, Jack turned to leave.

"Wait," Zooey cried, just as he crossed the threshold.

"Somebody else I forgot to say goodbye to?" he asked sarcastically. The woman was definitely getting under his skin and he needed to put distance between them. Before he did something that was going to cost him.

To his surprise, Zooey was dashing toward the living room. "No," she called over her shoulder, "but you did forget something." The next moment, she was back at the front door with his briefcase in her hands. She held it out to him with an amused smile on her face. "Here, you might need this."

Jack wrapped his fingers around the handle, pulling it to him with a quick motion she hadn't expected. The momentum had her jerking forward. And suddenly, there was absolutely no space between them. Not for a toothpick, not even for a sliver of air.

The foyer grew warmer.

Zooey could feel her heart accelerating just a touch as she looked up at him. Something threatened to melt inside her, as it always did when she stopped thinking of him as Emily and Jackie's father, or her boss, and saw him at the most basic level—a very good-looking man who did, on those occasions when she let her guard drop, take her breath away.

It was so still, she could hear her pulse vibrating in her ears.

"Wouldn't want you to go into the office without your briefcase," she finally said, doing her best to sound glib. Not an easy feat when all the moisture had suddenly evaporated from her mouth.

Damn it, it had happened again, Jack thought, annoyed with himself. From out of nowhere, riding on a lightning bolt, that same strong sense of attraction to her had materialized, just as it already had several times before. Each time, it felt as if a little more of his resolve was chipped away.

He had no idea why it overwhelmed him, when other times he could go along regarding her as his children's supernanny, a woman who somehow seemed to get everything done and not break a sweat. A woman his children seemed to adore and who could, thank God, calm them down even in their rowdiest moments.

All he knew was that every so often, every single pulse point in his body suddenly became aware of her as a woman. A very attractive woman.

He took a breath, trying not to appear as if his lungs had suddenly and mysteriously been depleted of the last ounce of oxygen.

"No, can't have that," he murmured, then nodded his head. "Thanks."

She smiled that odd little smile of hers, the one that quirked up in one corner. The one he wanted to kiss off her lips.

"Don't mention it."

Jack merely grunted, then turned and walked quickly to the safe haven of the garage. He never looked back. Even so, he knew she was watching him.

She made him feel like a kid. The last thing he should be feeling, given the responsibilities weighing so heavily on his shoulders.

Damn it, what was wrong with him? He shouldn't be letting himself react to her.

But he had. And not for the first time.

This was going to be a problem, Jack thought, getting into his BMW. He couldn't act on his feelings. For the first time since Patricia had died, his children appeared to be happy. And thriving. If he gave in to the flash of desire—damn, it had been desire, he admitted with exasperation—and things went badly, what would he do? He hadn't the first idea how to conduct a successful relationship. He had no blueprints to follow, no natural ability of his own—Patricia had been the first to point that out to him.

Once things *did* turn sour between himself and Zooey, he mused, recapturing his train of thought, he'd be out one perfect nanny. And right back where he'd been in January, when he'd first asked Zooey to watch the kids.

No, whatever was going on inside of him would have to remain there, swirling and twisting, and he was just going to have to deal with it.

Heaven knew, he thought, driving away from his house and Danbury Way, dealing with "it" was a lot easier than sitting and interviewing another endless parade of less than perfect nannies.

Out of the blue, the realization hit him right between the eyes.

My God, he'd almost kissed her back there.

What the hell was the matter with him? Jack upbraided himself.

Sex, that was what was the matter with him, he decided. Sex. Or, more accurately, lack thereof.

Jack swerved to avoid a car that was drifting into his lane, coming from the opposite direction. He swore roundly under his breath, feeling as if someone was pushing him onto a very thin tightrope.

Or maybe that was just the pent-up hormones doing the talking.

He hadn't been with a woman since Patricia was killed. And hadn't been with her in a while, either, except for that one time that resulted in Jackie.

No wonder he felt so tense, Jack realized. He was an average male who had hormones roaming through his body like midnight looters. He needed an outlet.

For a second, as he approached the end of the long cul-de-sac, he all but came to a stop. It occurred to him just what he needed.

It was, God help him, a date. He needed to spend time with a woman who would take his mind off Zooey.

Glancing into his rearview mirror, he saw Rebecca Peters standing outside her house. And she, as she turned around, saw him. Or at least his car.

The wide smile was unmistakable.

And it was also, he thought, a sign.

But one, he told himself, he was going to have to deal with later. Right now, he had a case to pull together.

"My stomach aches," Emily complained half an hour later as she sat at the breakfast table, staring into her bowl of cereal. The little girl pressed her lips together as if to keep from crying. "Can I stay home from school today?"

This was not the first time Emily had complained of a stomachache. There had been a number of other ailments cited as well, deployed as valid reasons for not going to school.

Zooey felt a slight tug on her heart. It brought back memories of early school days and those harsh feelings of not quite fitting in.

Glancing toward Jackie to make sure the

boy was still securely belted into his high chair, she drew her chair closer to Emily's and sat down. "Do you have a test today?"

Avoiding her eyes, Emily continued to stare into her bowl and shook her head. "No."

Zooey took another stab, although she had a feeling she knew what lay at the bottom of Emily's sudden maladies. "A book report due?"

"Did it," Emily told the sinking golden balls of cereal in her bowl. "Miss Nelson says it's due next Friday."

Zooey looked at her closer. "Somebody picking on you in school?"

Emily's frown grew deeper. Sadder. She raised the spoon, only to tilt it and watch the milk and little golden balls go cascading back into the bowl.

"No."

There was too much hesitation, Zooey thought. She was on the right trail. "Are you sure nobody's teasing you?" she coaxed gently. "Emily, you can tell me. I want to help."

The little girl raised her head, and Zooey saw the glimmer of tears as she fought them back. "Nobody's teasing me, Zooey. They don't even see me. They're like Daddy. I'm not even there."

Wow, and wasn't that a mouthful? But at least they'd reached the heart of it. Big time. Emily was suffering from a case of loneliness—on all fronts, it appeared. She thought her dad was ignoring her, and nobody had time for a shy little girl at school.

Time for a change, Zooey decided.

She put her arm around the girl. Emily laid her head against her shoulder. Moved, Zooey stroked the child's silky hair with her free hand. If she had a little girl, she thought, she'd look like this. Like Emily. Small and delicate. And vulnerable.

She was going to change the last part, Zooey promised herself. "Sure they see you, honey. And I bet they're wondering why you won't talk to them."

Emily raised her head, her eyes frightened. "Talk to them? What'll I say?"

"Well, 'hi' for openers." Zooey thought for a moment, trying to remember what it was like being seven. "If they're playing a game, you could ask to join in."

"I don't know any games," Emily murmured. "The nannies Daddy hired kept us in the house. They said it was easier than following Daddy's rules."

Ah, yes, Zooey thought. *Daddy's rules*. The

very same rules she completely disregarded. For an absent parent, the man had a myriad of rules to take the edge off his guilt. He was going to have to learn that it didn't work that way.

And, when it came to going out, she had noticed a certain reluctance, at least on Emily's part. The little girl seemed to be happiest sitting in front of the television set, a video game control pad in her hand. Since she'd heard that playing video games helped improve dexterity and hand-eye coordination, Zooey hadn't protested too much.

But it was definitely time to make a few changes.

Zooey thought of the kids in the house directly across the street. There were two boys and a girl living there—Anthony, who was nine, Michael, five, and Olivia, age seven— Emily's age. They belonged to Angela Schumacher, a single mom who worked as an office manager. The woman was a regular supermom, to the extent that when her younger sister, Megan, needed a place to stay, she'd taken her in as well.

But it was Olivia Zooey was interested in at the moment.

"Emily," she began slowly, "aren't you in the same class as Olivia—?"

Emily abandoned her cereal and looked up at Zooey, puzzled. "Yes."

"Do you like Olivia?" Zooey asked her innocently.

Emily nodded, her blond hair bobbing. "Everyone likes Olivia." There was a wistful note in the little girl's voice.

All systems are go, Zooey thought. Now they just had to wait for liftoff. She nodded at the bowl of cereal. "You about done with that?"

"Uh-huh." Emily pushed the bowl of soggy golden balls to the center of the table. "My stomach hurts," she repeated.

"We're going to fix that stomach," Zooey promised. Getting up, she crossed to Jackie and unstrapped him from the high chair. He all but bounced up, pivoting on the footrest and straining for freedom.

This boy has too much energy, Zooey thought. Lifting him out of the chair, she felt his legs immediately begin to wave back and forth as if he was attempting to propel himself upward.

All things considered, Zooey decided that

it was more prudent to hang on to the boy than to set him down. She tucked him against her hip.

"You're riding in style right now, fella." She turned toward his sister. "Emily, go get your backpack."

"Now?" she asked, even as she hurried to the corner by the counter where she had deposited her backpack on the way into the kitchen.

"Yes, now." Zooey grabbed her purse and slung the strap over her shoulder as she led the way to the front door.

"But we're early," Emily cried. This was definitely *not* what she had in mind. She wanted to avoid school, not get there early.

"We're not going to school just yet," Zooey told her. She held the door open, then locked it behind them. Pocketing her key, she by-passed the car in the driveway and continued walking. "First we have to make a stop at the house across the street."

Emily scrunched up her face, completely confused as she hurried to keep up with her nanny and her brother. "Why?"

"We're going to ask Olivia's mom if she'd like us to take Olivia to school with us."

"Olivia?" Emily repeated the name with hushed reverence. "In our car?"

"Why not?" Zooey stopped just shy of the neighbor's front door and looked at Emily, a whimsical smile playing on her lips. "Does she have cooties?"

Emily's face scrunched up again as she desperately tried to follow the conversation. "What's that?"

Zooey merely shook her head. Boy, things certainly changed a lot. Fast.

"Sorry, wrong generation, I guess." And then, because Emily was still looking up at her with a quizzical expression on her face, she explained, "Cooties are something that boys say girls have so they don't have to play with them."

Emily frowned, looking at her little brother. Jackie made a face at her, then laughed, secure in the sanctuary provided by Zooey's arms. "Boys are stupid."

Zooey laughed. "I'm sure your father will appreciate you holding that thought until you're at least thirty. Maybe older."

Standing in front of Angela Schumacher's door, Zooey shifted Jackie to her other hip and rang the doorbell. A minute or so later, she was about to ring a second time when the door finally opened.

She expected to see Olivia's mother in the doorway. Instead, it was Megan.

Even better, Zooey thought. She had gotten friendly with Olivia's aunt.

"Oh, hi." Megan's gaze swept over Zooey, taking in Jackie and Emily. She seemed mildly surprised to see them at this hour. "Are you looking for Angela?" Even as she asked, Megan glanced over her shoulder into the house.

Zooey stopped her before she could call out to her sister. "No, actually, we're looking for Olivia."

Turning back, Megan glanced at the little girl who was all but hiding behind Zooey. She smiled at her. Painfully shy, Emily shifted even farther behind Zooey. "My niece?"

"Yes. I thought that since both Olivia and Emily here—" she nodded at the child, who was attempting to morph into her own shadow "—go to the same school—"

"The same class," Emily told her in a stage whisper. "Miss Nelson's, remember?"

"Sorry," Zooey replied in the same stage whisper. "The same class," she said in a normal voice to Megan, "we thought we'd ask if your sister would like us to take Olivia to school with us this morning."

Megan looked a little taken aback by the unexpected offer. "Um, sure. I don't see why not." She held up her finger, as if to pause the action. "Just let me go and ask her. Come in, won't you?"

Zooey nodded and stepped in the door, Jackie still in her arms. Emily was right there behind them, clinging to the hem of Zooey's jacket.

Megan disappeared, calling out to Angela, loudly repeating the offer that had just been made.

It was a nice house, Zooey thought, looking around. But it felt a little lonely.

Both Megan and Angela appeared in less than two minutes. Olivia was between them, striding to keep up with the adults.

"Thank you," Angela said warmly. "Your offer is much appreciated." She flushed slightly. "I'm running behind this morning."

Zooey smiled. "Isn't everyone? Emily, why don't you take Olivia to the car? I'll be there in a second."

As Emily shyly took Olivia's hand and led her outside, Zooey turned toward Angela and quickly explained the sudden request for a carpool.

This morning was going to mark the beginning of the end of Emily's painful shyness.

Chapter Five

It dawned on Zooey in the middle of a left turn fifteen minutes later that she was beginning to have definite parentlike feelings when it came to dealing with the Lever children. Especially Emily.

These last few months she'd become closer to the little girl, ached for her when she seemed to be so alone or when Emily longed for her father to pay some attention to her. Zooey had become acutely aware of just what her own mother must have gone through raising *her*.

Of how her mom must have felt. And what had been going through her mother's mind when she'd wanted her to join the family firm.

Zooey had never thought of either of her parents as particularly bad people. She'd never felt rage, or gone through that I-hate-you period that some teenagers experienced, turning life into a living hell for themselves and their parents.

But she hadn't exactly been the easiest person to get along with, either. Admittedly, the last few years she'd been perverse, saying "day" when her parents and Uncle Andrew had said "night" just because she didn't want to be agreeable. Didn't want to walk the same path they walked. The one they wanted her to take.

She still didn't want to be part of the family business, but it suddenly dawned on her that her parents hadn't pushed for it because they wanted to be mean or didn't care about her dreams. They just wanted what they thought was the best for her.

Zooey's epiphany inside the silver SUV brought with it a slash of guilt that came equipped with big, sharp teeth. Said teeth took a sizable chunk out of her. There were words she did regret saying, people she did regret hurting.

She supposed that part of the trouble was that she knew, despite her seemingly breezy attitude, that she'd never thought she would measure up to what was expected of her. And, coming from two parents who were as close to perfect as was possible, she hadn't wanted to disappoint them. The best way to avoid certain disappointment was not to try in the first place. Not to get involved in what they wanted her to be involved in.

So she'd chucked it all—school, Connor, everything—in order to avoid presenting them with the ultimate disappointment: a daughter who was a failure on all fronts.

In its own circular way, that made sense to her. But probably not to anyone else.

"Sorry, Mom," she murmured under her breath, just as she glanced in the rearview mirror.

Emily was sitting in the middle of the backseat, with Jackie strapped into his car seat on one side and Olivia belted in on her other, directly behind the driver's seat.

Emily, Zooey noted, no longer had that distant-because-I'm-scared expression on her face. Good. She'd even heard Emily say a few words to Olivia. What was more important, Olivia had said a few words back. And they hadn't sounded as if they'd been squeezed out of the clogged end of a used tube of toothpaste. They had flowed freely. So freely that within a few minutes, Olivia began to chatter. And soon there was an actual conversation going on back there.

Zooey smiled to herself.

They were making progress. And it was probably a toss-up as to who was happier about it—her or Emily. Maybe it was a tie, Zooey thought, her smile spreading into a wide grin.

"Hey, Olivia?" Zooey raised her voice in order to be heard above the din. Politely, Olivia immediately stopped talking to listen. She'd chosen a good playmate for Emily, Zooey thought, congratulating herself. "Emily and I are thinking of going shopping this weekend."

"Shopping?" Olivia uttered the word with reverence and wistfulness.

"You know, for some new clothes for the fall." Not risking turning around, Zooey raised her eyes to the mirror again. Emily appeared surprised, but Olivia was fairly beaming. "Think you and your mom or your aunt Megan might be interested in joining us?"

As of yet, Emily hadn't developed any particular interest in acquiring new clothing.

Zooey had a strong hunch that Olivia, even at this young, tender age, was a shopper.

The sparkle in the child's eyes told her she'd guessed correctly. "Sure," Olivia cried enthusiastically. "I'll ask my mom," she promised, then turned to Emily. "But she'll say yes. I know she will."

Emily nodded. Things were happening a little too fast for her to assimilate. She'd never had a friend before, other than her brother. But slowly, a smile slipped across her lips.

Zooey saw it and felt a surge of triumph. "Okay, then we'll consider it a date," she said to Olivia.

Now all she had to do, Zooey thought as she approached the school, was get Jack to sign off on this.

For once, Jack was getting home earlier than he'd expected. Or at least he'd left the office earlier than he'd been doing for the last few weeks.

He felt drained and yet wired. Wired because the morning's near-miss with Zooey hadn't quite faded from his mind, despite all the effort he'd put into forgetting it since he'd driven away from his house. Something seemed to be stirring inside of him. Something he didn't want stirring.

But he couldn't exactly go into hiding, either. He lived here, for God's sake. A man shouldn't feel uneasy coming home at night. Uneasy not because of what was waiting for him, but because of what he might be tempted to do.

As he turned the corner onto his street, he saw Bo Conway working on the car that stood in the driveway of Carly Anderson's house.

Bo's house pretty soon, Jack thought.

The house had been dubbed the McMansion by the other residents of Danbury Way because, for one thing, it was almost twice the size of the other homes on the block.

When Carly and her ex-husband moved in, the house had been like all the others along the cul-de-sac. And then they had bought the house next door as well because Carly wanted to merge the two houses together to create one great big one.

Bo Conway had been the last contractor on the scene, coming in to augment and tinker with the McMansion at the tail end of Carly's crumbling marriage. He'd stayed on to offer a shoulder to cry on. And that turned into an offer to love, honor and cherish. Or words to that effect.

The words themselves would be uttered soon, Jack knew, because what Bo had ultimately repaired was Carly's broken heart and very damaged self-esteem. When her husband suddenly declared that he was leaving because he was no longer in love with her, Carly Anderson's entire world had crashed and burned. She had, according to rumor, lost all hope, all faith that life held anything for her but emptiness. Amid all the wealth she had surrounded herself with, she was very poor.

But Bo had fixed all that, Jack thought as he pulled his BMW into the driveway and set the hand brake.

Too bad there wasn't some kind of magic around to fix him, he mused. Because he felt he was just as much a member of the walking wounded as Carly had been.

Except that he wasn't able to divert himself by adding on to the house or turning bedrooms into dens. His answer, he knew, was to work. Because work was something he was good at. Life, apparently, was not. His marriage had been doomed even before the accident. Oh, he'd had all sorts of hopes when he'd married Patricia. Delusional hopes, he now realized.

He had absolutely no idea how to love someone, how to conduct a satisfying and satisfactory relationship. There were no examples to follow in his life, no blueprints to emulate. He hadn't a clue.

All he knew was work. So he'd buried himself in it again, only to be told that he was shortchanging his kids.

Getting out of his car, Jack called out a greeting to Bo. The tall, muscular, brown-haired man was everything he wasn't, Jack thought—warm, friendly, outgoing. And, from what he'd heard, Bo came from a close-knit family. Jack had no idea how that felt, what that meant. To him, "close" meant standing next to one another—certainly not sharing feelings or fears or thoughts, all of which he now found himself unable to do.

It was a sad, vicious cycle. God, but he envied Bo.

About to walk into his house, Jack was surprised when the man waved him over. Welcoming the diversion, Jack crossed the yard to the McMansion and nodded at Bo, who was doing something with the car he was working on that Jack wouldn't have understood if his life depended on it.

"Hi, what's up?"

Bo wiped his hands on the back of his jeans, his biceps rippling as he did so.

I've got to get back to the gym, Jack thought.

Coming closer, Bo asked in a low voice, "Can you keep a secret?"

Jack thought it was an odd question. They were friends, granted, but it wasn't exactly as if they'd become close. Still, he felt a little pleased at being approached.

"I'm a lawyer," Jack reminded him. "I'm supposed to be closemouthed."

Bo grinned, inclining his head. "Yeah, but this doesn't exactly come under the heading of attorney-client privilege."

Jack saw his point. He nodded and said, rather solemnly, not knowing what to expect, "Yes, I can keep a secret."

Bo looked around, just in case someone was listening, but for once, and probably only for a moment, Danbury Way was devoid of people, young or old. "Carly and I are getting married."

Jack laughed. "Hate to rain on your parade, but that's not much of a secret, Bo. Everyone around here kind of suspected that."

Bo shook his head. "No, I mean next week." He lowered his voice even more, although it was obvious he found it hard to contain his enthusiasm. "We're eloping."

"Eloping?" Jack repeated the word skeptically. "Are you sure Carly wants that?"

Bo was a down-to-earth kind of guy, but everyone knew Carly liked all the trimmings. If something could be done on a small scale or a grand one, she'd choose grand every time. According to what Patricia had once told him, twelve bridesmaids had been in attendance at Carly's wedding to Greg. Jack fully expected there to be fourteen this time around.

But Bo seemed to have other ideas. "Definitely. Carly said she wants this to be as different from her first wedding as possible. It's going to be just her, me and a preacher to make it legal. And a couple of witnesses off the street," he said. "Would you mind looking after the place while we're gone? I've installed a great security system, but you never know. Burglars always seem to be one step ahead."

Jack thought it odd that Bo should ask him instead of Molly Jackson or Rebecca Peters, the people who lived in the houses on either side of Carly's. But then, he supposed that Bo felt more comfortable asking a guy to look after things.

"I'm not around that much, but sure, I'll keep an eye out for you when I'm here. I can get Zooey to pick up the mail and hold on to it until you two get back." It occurred to him that he was volunteering Zooey's services as if they were a set, and hoped that Bo didn't get any wrong ideas.

But Bo seemed too blissfully happy to notice. "Perfect." He nodded, pleased. "Knew I could count on you. I'd offer to bring you back a souvenir from Maui, but I don't think Carly and I will be leaving the hotel room very much." Bo grinned broadly as he looked at him. "There's nothing like being in love, Jack."

"I really wouldn't know," Jack murmured.

"That's because all you do is work." Bo hit the back of his hand against Jack's chest, as if to remind him that there was a heart there whose function was to do more than just pump blood. "You really need to get out more often, buddy."

Jack knew Bo meant well. People who were in love wanted the rest of the world to join them, but the last thing he wanted was roman-

tic advice. In his case it was as useless as offering a pair of earmuffs to a frog.

"Yeah, well…" His voice trailed off.

Bo apparently wasn't about to let the matter drop so easily. "I'm sure Rebecca wouldn't
mind if you asked her out."

"Rebecca?" He wasn't a man who noticed
women looking at him, but he would have
had to be blind not to notice the interest in
the freelance photographer's eyes whenever
their paths crossed.

"Sure." Bo nodded toward the woman's
house. After him, Rebecca was the "new
kid" on the block, having moved here from
New York City, and she stuck out like a sore
thumb. She moved fast, talked fast and was
in general fast. "Haven't you noticed the way
that woman all but drools whenever you drive
by?" Bo winked. "Try walking by instead.
As a matter of fact, I know she's home now.
I saw her car pull up less than twenty minutes ago. Why don't you stop by, ask her out
for coffee sometime."

This was going a lot faster than Jack was
comfortable with. "I don't know…"

But Bo was not about to let him back away.
"That's just the point. You can't know, until
you do something about it. You know what

they say—all work and no play makes Jack a dull boy."

Jack had never liked that cliché. Besides, he wasn't sure if he actually wanted to go out with Rebecca. Oh, the woman was extremely attractive in a smoldering, sexy sort of way, but when he came right down to it, that wasn't really his type.

Hell, he didn't know what his type was. Lately he'd found himself feeling attracted to Zooey—the nanny, for heaven's sake. It wasn't as if his experience had taken him far and wide. Once he'd left high school behind, there'd only been Patricia. He'd always been too busy trying to make something of himself to go the partying route in college. After graduation, he'd really buckled down.

Bo picked up the two rags he'd dropped on the ground and placed them on the hood of the car. "Since you seem to have lead in your feet, why don't I just walk you over there?"

Jack stared at him. "And I do what—knock on her door and ask her out?"

The look on Bo's face said he expected him to do exactly that. "Sure, why not? Hey, Jack, it's done all the time."

He had no doubt that it was, yet that didn't

make him comfortable with the notion. "Maybe, but not by me."

Bo looked at him seriously. "Maybe it's time to start."

"If I run into her, perhaps," Jack allowed. "But if I have to go to her house, then no, it doesn't seem casual enough. I—"

Bo was looking at something over his shoulder. And grinning. "Guess what."

"What?" But even as he asked, Jack had a feeling he knew exactly what was coming.

Putting his hand on Jack's shoulder, Bo turned him around.

While they'd been talking, Rebecca had come out of her house. She was standing on her porch, hands on her hips as she scanned the area. The crisp fall wind was weaving sensuously through her hair.

Bo inclined his head toward Jack, so his voice wouldn't carry. "She just stepped out of her house. Casual enough for you?" And then he straightened, looking pleased. "It's fate, man," he assured him. "Nothing less than fate stepping in."

Maybe it was at that, Jack thought. After all, hadn't he been thinking about some sort of a diversion, something to get his mind off Zooey's being anything more than a fantastic nanny? If he started seeing someone else, then maybe that would take the edge off the way he was feeling. Maybe those damn "stirrings" that were going on in his gut would subside and disappear.

It was worth a try.

Zooey looked toward the door for possibly the tenth time in as many minutes. It was still not moving, still not opening. She sighed.

She was certain she'd heard Jack's car pull up in the driveway a full ten minutes ago, but there was no sign of him yet. What was taking him so long? She didn't want to seem as if she was standing around, listening for the sound of his car, but on the other hand, what if something was wrong? What if he was sitting out there, wrestling with something he wanted to say to her?

There'd definitely been something humming between them this morning. Neither one of them had acted on it, but it had been there.

Had it put him off? Made him reconsider having her live on the premises? Or was he just being a typical male, not knowing how to react?

Or was it something simpler than that? Did it have to do with the kids? Had she been too pushy this morning, all but marching him up the stairs to say goodbye to Emily and Jackie? She wondered if he expected her to apologize for that.

Zooey chewed on her lower lip, thinking. She couldn't very well apologize to the man for wanting him to take a more active role in his kids' lives. As their nanny, she was *supposed* to have their best interests at heart.

Damn it, where *was* he?

She had an excuse, she told herself, to go to the window and look for him. She wanted to tell him about the progress Emily had made today and about the proposed shopping trip this Saturday.

Her mouth curved in a smile. Technically, she did need his permission for that, especially since she was going to be spending his money on Emily's new fall wardrobe.

Zooey blew out a breath and headed for the door with long, purposeful strides. She was just about to pull it open when she heard a key being inserted in the lock. The next second, the door opened and Jack walked in.

"Hi." She offered him a sunny smile, taking his briefcase from him and placing it at the base of the coatrack, the way he always did when he first walked in. "You're home early. Taking my advice? Or did your firm suddenly run out of clients?"

"Neither." He shrugged out of the light top-coat he had on, hanging it up. "Court got out early."

"Hungry?" She was already turning toward the kitchen. "I made pot roast."

That was what was different, he realized. It was quiet. Whenever he came home early—in Jack's world, that meant anytime before 7:00 p.m.—it took exactly five seconds before he was surrounded by short people. But there was no sound of running feet, no greetings of "Daddy!" echoing through the air.

He looked at Zooey. "Where are the kids?"

"Jackie fell asleep right after dinner, so I put him to bed." She smiled fondly. "Emily is still at Olivia's house."

He tried to place the name and couldn't. "Who's Olivia?"

"The little girl across the street. Her mother's Angela Schumacher. Her aunt's Megan Schumacher, the woman Greg Banning is seeing. Carly Anderson's ex," she added for good measure.

Zooey certainly kept up on the neighborhood gossip a lot more than he did. And then he replayed her words in his head. "Emily's at someone else's house?" Since when did that happen?

"She's playing," Zooey declared triumphantly. She backtracked a little. "Haven't you noticed how shy Emily is?"

His shrug was careless. "She's a little girl." As far as he knew, because he had no experience, all little girls were shy.

Zooey laughed. The man needed to have his stereotypes updated. "Don't know many little girls, do you? They're shy for a minute and a half, until they get to know you, then they're live wires. Emily's precocious and she makes a lot of waves at home, but when it comes to being around girls her own age, she is *pain*fully *shy*."

He didn't follow. "So what's she doing at someone else's house?"

Zooey paused to fluff up a pillow that had been flattened earlier by Jackie. "Hopefully, getting over her shyness. I volunteered to take Olivia to school today. They're in the same class," she added, guessing that he probably wouldn't know that. "After school, they did their homework together here, had dinner together and then went to Olivia's to play." It was hard to keep the note of triumph out of her voice. So far, things were going swimmingly. "And, this coming Saturday, the four of us are going out to shop."

"Shop?" He frowned. He would rather endure a root canal. "I can't go shopping."

She was getting ahead of herself. "Sorry, not the four of *us*—" she vaguely pointed to him and then herself "—the four of us. Emily, Olivia, her aunt Megan and me," she elaborated.

He was probably going to have to go into the office at some point Saturday. He couldn't do that if no one was home to watch his son. "What about Jackie?"

"Arrangements are being made," Zooey assured him complacently. She wasn't about to tell him that she was planning on asking her mother to watch the boy, not until she was certain it was possible. She hadn't spoken to her mother in over ten months, just before she'd taken that job at the coffee shop. They'd had a huge fight over it and Zooey had stormed out of the house.

She regretted that now.

She cocked her head, looking at Jack curiously. "You sounded adamant about not being able to go with us. Is it just the typical male phobia about malls and shopping in general, or are they chaining you to the courthouse over the weekend?"

"Neither. Actually, I do have to do some work in the early afternoon, and after that…" Jack paused, searching for the right words to phrase this, then told himself he was being ridiculous. What he did or didn't do with his social life shouldn't matter one way or another to Zooey. She was just making conversation. "I have a date Saturday night."

It was one of the very few times in her life that Zooey found herself at a loss for words.

Chapter Six

It took her several very long seconds before she could locate her tongue, and several more before she could get it in gear well enough to form words. The numbness that had descended over her body felt like an encasing plastic garment bag, sucking away her air.

"A date?"

"Yes. With Rebecca Peters." Even as he said it, he was having doubts. Had he just allowed himself to be railroaded into something? Or was this the only course he could take, under the extenuating circumstances he found himself grappling with?

Zooey continued to stare at him. When had all this happened? "From down the block?"

"Yes." If he'd ever been more uncomfortable in his life, Jack would have been hard-pressed to remember when. "Is that a problem?"

Yes, it's a problem, you big, dumb jerk. "No." She forced a smile to her lips. "Why should it be a problem?" God, but her voice sounded hollow. *Why aren't you asking me out if you feel the need to go out with someone?*

"No reason, you just looked like—" Jack shook his head.

He'd thought she looked upset, but maybe he was projecting his own feelings onto her. He didn't want her to think that he felt she was attracted to him. It was the other way around that was the problem.

He cleared his throat, desperately searching for something to send the conversation in another direction. "You said something about pot roast?"

Yes, how'd you like to wear it? She'd hoped, as little as a few minutes ago, that they could enjoy a quiet meal together. Now her appetite had completely vanished.

"It's in the kitchen. I'm going to go get Emily," she murmured.

She didn't mean to slam the front door as she left; the handle just slipped out of her hand.

Hands clenched at her sides, more from anger than the nippy October evening and the fact that she'd left the house wearing only her pullover sweater, Zooey made her way across the street.

As she went down the walk, she heard very distinct, plaintive cries: Jackie was waking up from his premature nap. She could almost visualize the distressed look on Jack's face.

Zooey just kept walking. *Good, call your girlfriend and ask her to handle that.*

Despite her enthusiasm and zest, Zooey had always been a good poker player, able to maintain an expressionless mask on her face even when holding a winning hand. And that skill was coming in handy now. There was no way she was going to let Jack see that his newly invigorated social life had any effect on her at all.

So instead, she went about life for the next three days as if he hadn't dropped a bomb on her. As if she didn't want to do the same, literally, on number 4 Danbury Way, where Rebecca Peters had taken up residence.

Even so, it took everything Zooey had to keep her temper in check and to go about business as usual. For one thing, it wasn't as usual. Jack was going out. He had a date. With someone else.

Damn it.

She'd hoped, fantasized, that when the time came that Jack Lever could be torn away from his court cases and his legal briefs, she'd be the one he'd do the tearing for, not some brown-haired, blue-eyed, curvy ex-fashion magazine contributor.

She'd been fooling herself, she supposed, but damn it, she'd felt certain that there was chemistry between them. Was positive when he looked at her, he felt the same way.

Get with the program, Zooey, she upbraided herself. Jack Lever's social calendar wasn't supposed to be the dominant thing in her life. She had responsibilities, things to do.

She blew out a breath. Right now she needed to confirm that Saturday's shopping trip was a "go."

Pressing her lips together, Zooey looked up at the five-story building she was parked in front of. The building that housed the corporate offices of Finnegan's Fine Furniture.

She couldn't put this off any longer. She could take Jackie tomorrow, but that would definitely put a crimp in Emily's day, and the little girl deserved to enjoy it without having her rambunctious brother in tow. Although Zooey loved Jackie as if he were her own, she knew he could be one huge pain when he wanted to be.

Not for nothing did they call it the terrible twos, she thought.

Zooey frowned. Time to get with it.

She turned in her seat to look at the little boy in the car seat behind her. "Well, I guess we can't stay here all morning, huh?"

"No," Jackie declared, using his newly acquired favorite word.

She laughed at him, shaking her head, then turned around again and looked back at the building as she released her seat belt. How had so much time managed to slip by? she wondered, still mentally dragging her feet.

"Okay, here goes nothing."

"No."

"Easy for you to say."

With her fingers on the door handle, ready to open it, she still hung back a second longer.

This was a first, she supposed. She'd never felt nervous before, not about seeing her own mother. But then, she had never teetered on the edge of estrangement, either.

Getting out of the car, Zooey rounded the back and went to the rear passenger side, where Jackie sat strapped in his car seat.

It was chilly this morning, she thought, hunching her shoulders. Or maybe she just felt cold because she was nervous.

The second she opened the door, Jackie's waving feet went into double time. He really wanted to get out, Zooey realized. "Settle down, Jackie," she soothed.

The feet went faster as he grinned, looking like an angelic little devil. "No!"

She sighed. "Have it your way."

Unbuckling him, she took the boy out and planted him firmly on her hip. She knew that taking his hand and having him walk on his own would have been better for the boy, but she was in a hurry, and the only time those little legs of his pumped fast was when he was fleeing the scene of his latest crime.

Zooey walked through the front door of the building and looked slowly around the lobby. There were a handful of paintings on the wall.

It looked, she thought, just as she remembered it. Of course, not a whole lot of time had gone by, but somehow, part of her had expected that it would look different. Because she *felt* different. Wiser.

She nodded to the guard at the front desk and crossed to the elevator. She could tell by the old man's expression that he was trying to place her and was unsuccessful. She hadn't exactly been a regular visitor here even when things had been going fairly well at home.

When she'd actually thought she had a shot at being the person she felt everyone in the family wanted her to be.

The elevator car arrived and she stepped into it. A second later, it was time to step off again. The aluminum doors opened onto a plush, airy second floor. There was a receptionist sitting at a desk that seemed to run half the length of the hall.

It all looked so classy. She could remember when everything had been operated from their garage. She couldn't have been more than Emily's age. Seventeen years had brought about a lot of changes.

Her parents had done very well for themselves, she realized. The rush of pride was a surprise, and she savored it.

"Excuse me, do you have an appointment?"

the young woman called as Zooey walked right by her toward the offices in the rear of the building.

"Don't need one," Zooey stated over her shoulder.

"No," Jackie sang out.

"You tell her, kid," she laughed.

The receptionist was on her feet immediately, hurrying after her. "Wait," she cried. "You can't go in there without an appointment."

Zooey made it to her mother's office door and smiled to herself. For a young thing, she certainly wasn't in very good shape, Zooey thought.

"Mrs. Finnegan, I'm sorry," the young woman panted breathlessly, "but she—"

Frances Finnegan looked up from the computer monitor and last quarter's financial statements that she was reviewing. Surprise washed through her as the sight of her daughter registered. Zooey was the last person she'd expected to see walking in. And what was she doing with a baby?

She looked at the child carefully. There was no resemblance. Not to Zooey, or to any of her other children when they were that age. Did he look like his father?

Had Zooey gotten married to a man with a ready-made family?

"That's all right, Liz." Frances slowly rose to her feet, her eyes never leaving her daughter and the little boy riding her hip. As an afterthought, Frances waved the receptionist away. "This is my daughter, Zooey."

"Oh." The woman looked as if she could have been knocked over with a sneeze. "Then it's all right," she murmured, backing away.

"Is it?" Zooey asked, gazing at her mother. Her mom made no answer as the receptionist left, closing the door. "You look good, Mom."

"You look thin," Frances responded. "You're not eating enough." It wasn't a criticism, it was an observation. By now, she was standing in front of Zooey. "May I?" she asked.

"Sure. Careful," she cautioned as her mother took Jackie into her arms, "he's a live wire."

Frances glanced at her daughter. She did love Zooey. Very much. And she'd missed her these past months. It had almost killed her to give Zooey the space she'd wanted. "And you weren't?"

Zooey shrugged carelessly. "I can't remember that far back."

"Trust me," Frances assured her, her voice

now warm, "you were." A wide smile replaced the cautious look. "What's his name?"

"Jackie. Jack Jr. John, Junior, really," Zooey corrected. Since Jack never used his legal name, she tended to forget what was actually entered on their birth certificates.

Frances nodded. It had been a long time since she'd held a child in her arms. Every maternal bone in her body woke up and rejoiced at the contact with this soft bundle of perpetual motion. She made the boy comfortable against her. He cuddled close and she savored the feeling.

"Jackie," Frances repeated. The little boy began to wiggle again in response to his name. "Hi, Jackie," she murmured with a smile. She looked up at her daughter again. "Whose is he? Not yours, right?"

There was a hint of longing in her mother's voice. Zooey felt a smattering of guilt. Had she married Connor the way her parents had both hoped, she might have been well on her way to giving them their first grandchild.

Zooey banished the thought from her brain. No point in thinking about things that mercifully never came to pass.

"No, he's not mine." She stroked the boy's hair. It was getting rather long, she thought, absently. Time for a haircut soon. "I'm just responsible for him."

There was no emotion in Frances's voice, but her eyes gave her away. "You're babysitting now?"

Long ago, when she'd left college, Zooey had tried to make peace with the fact that she was going to be a disappointment to her parents. Still, it hurt to be in the same room as that disappointment, to see it take form.

"It's a little more professional-sounding than that, Mom. I'm a nanny."

"A nanny," Frances echoed. "With a near-genius IQ." She supposed it was a step up from dog walking, and tied with waitressing, but when she thought of the hopes she'd had for Zooey, the dreams...

Frances caught herself. This wasn't the way she wanted things to go with her daughter. "Sorry. I swore the next time I saw you, I wouldn't be judgmental." She looked down at Jackie. "Is this your way of trying to reconcile? Bringing me a baby to hold?"

"No baby!" Jackie declared.

Frances raised her eyes to Zooey's in barely suppressed amusement.

"He's two," Zooey told her with just a hint of exasperation.

Frances smiled, remembering. Relieved that those years were long gone. And yet, in hindsight, things had been simpler back then. And the world a great deal smaller.

She nodded, looking at the boy. "That would explain it."

Her mother was a natural at this, Zooey thought, watching her. Funny how she'd never realized that until now. "I was wondering if you could watch him for me."

"Now?" Her tone indicated that it wouldn't have been out of the question, even if the answer was yes.

"No," Zooey told her quickly. She peered at her mother's face. "It would be just for a few hours. This Saturday."

"Why me?"

"Because you're the best person for the job," Zooey told her honestly. There was more she needed to say. Years to apologize for. She wasn't sure just where to start. Taking a breath, she plunged in. "Look, Mom, I've been doing this for a while now—"

Curiosity got the better of Frances. "What's 'a while'?"

"Ten months." Her momentum breached, Zooey began again. "And it's taught me something."

Frances offered the keys to her Porsche to Jackie, who was immediately fascinated. His eyes sparkled as he took them in his chubby hands.

"Patience?" Frances guessed, looking over his head at her daughter.

"Among other things," Zooey allowed, veering back on track again. "Mainly it's taught me that you and Dad went through a lot raising me. Raising Kim and Ethan and Tyler, too," she added, lest her mother thought she was singling herself out. "And…" Oh, what the hell. She could go on for hours with this. In the interest of brevity, she got to the bottom line. "Look, Mom, I'm sorry."

Puzzled, Frances stopped making funny faces at Jackie, who was a very receptive audience, and looked up at her daughter. "Come again?"

"I'm sorry," Zooey repeated, this time with more feeling. "I'm sorry for the grief I gave you, and for all the hard times."

Frances could hardly believe what she was hearing. This didn't sound like her headstrong, stubborn daughter. She treaded lightly.

"Does this mean you're coming back? That you'll work in the business?"

That was a little further ahead than she'd intended on going right now.

Zooey smiled. "No. It means I don't want to be estranged anymore."

Shifting Jackie to her hip as easily as Zooey had, Frances laced her free arm around her daughter's shoulders, bringing her closer and kissing her forehead. "I never was. Your father and I just let you have that 'space' you kept clamoring for."

"And I appreciate it," Zooey told her honestly. "I also don't want as much of it as I thought I did." Her mother stared at her, surprised and pleased. "I know that you just want the best for me."

Jackie had latched on to her necklace. Gently, Frances disengaged his fingers and held them. She was nothing short of astounded at this epiphany her daughter had gone through. "That must be some job you have."

"It has its moments," she admitted.

Zooey went to take Jackie from her mother, thinking that she'd probably had enough for a first dose. To her surprise, she shook her head. Her mom had more endurance than she'd remembered.

After being cut off for over ten months,

Frances was hungry for details. "How many children are there?"

"Two." Zooey knew better than to say "just two." At times Emily and Jackie seemed more like an army. "Jackie and his sister, Emily. She's seven and very shy. I'm trying to get her to come around a little."

Frances shook her head. "Can't force these kinds of things."

"I know." Zooey was working from memory here, realizing what it was like to be seven. She couldn't remember what it was like to be shy because she'd never been that way a day in her life. "But there's a little girl across the street who's in Emily's class. I'm taking the two of them shopping tomorrow. That's why I need someone to watch the baby." She stroked Jackie's hair again.

"What's wrong with leaving him with his parents?" Frances asked matter-of-factly. Seemed to her that parents should want to spend time with the children they'd brought into the world. She'd had a career and still managed to make time for four children in various stages of growth. Never once did she think she was doing anything out of the ordinary. "I can't see them not wanting to be with this huggable sweetie."

"Parent," Zooey corrected. "There's only one."

She saw curiosity in her mother's eyes. "Divorced?"

Zooey shook her head. "Widower."

"So then you're working for a single father?" Frances asked with interest.

"Yes." She knew her mother. She needed to give Jack's credentials quickly before Frances Finnegan allowed her imagination to run wild. "He's a partner at a law firm—a criminal lawyer," she added, not knowing if that was a good thing in her mother's eyes.

A slight frown flickered across Frances's face. Obviously not a good thing, Zooey thought.

"I certainly hope he doesn't bring his work home."

Zooey sighed. "He rarely brings himself home."

Frances made the natural leap, given the information. "Then you live there?"

"Yes," Zooey said slowly, wondering if that was going to be a problem for her mother. She'd once thought of her mom as an extremely closed-minded woman—before she'd realized what it was like to worry about someone you cared about.

Jackie threw down the keys. Frances scooped them up and set them aside, jiggling the child ever so slightly to keep him quiet. It was second nature to her. "And what's this criminal lawyer's name?" she asked.

Oh, God, she wasn't going to sic a P. I. on Jack, was she? "Mom, don't get all maternal on me—"

Frances gave her a serene smile. "Isn't that why you came?"

Zooey paused. "I came to mend fences and to ask for help. Limited help," she stressed. "He's a very nice man, Mom."

Now just a hint of suspicion appeared in her eyes. "Exactly how nice?"

"Up to your standards nice," Zooey told her. And then, because she could see her mother needed a little more convincing, she added, "Like Connor, except without the greed."

Frances had always been quick to defend those she'd taken a liking to, and she was not yet disenchanted with her firstborn's ex-fiancé.

"Connor wasn't greedy."

"You never knew the real Connor, Mom." Zooey's engagement had long been a thing of the past, and she wanted to keep it that way. "But I didn't come here to talk about him—"

Frances looked at her. There was something Zooey needed to be told. "He's dating Kim, you know."

The information caught Zooey off guard. Kim had always been competitive, wanting everything her sister had. There were times when Zooey thought her sibling didn't have the sense to come out of the rain—not if she was trying to beat someone out. Zooey also knew that there was no way Kim would listen to anything she had to say.

Kim was at that age, Zooey realized. How did their mom stand it?

"Tell her to run for the hills," was Zooey's only comment. And then she smiled brightly, getting back to the reason for her visit. "So, will you do it? Will you watch Jackie for me tomorrow?"

"How could I say no to such a handsome young man?" Frances laughed, giving Jackie one last hug before she surrendered him back to Zooey. "Come to the house and leave him as long as you like." She paused for a moment before adding, "On one condition."

Zooey knew better than to say yes before

she knew all the details. Uncle Andrew had taught her that, too. "And that condition is?"

"You say hello to your father."

Well, that wasn't really a hardship, especially seeing as how she wanted to get back into the fold. "Done," Zooey declared.

Frances took the hand she offered and shook it. "Done."

Chapter Seven

"Look, Daddy, look!" Emily cried excitedly as she erupted through the door like a stick of TNT that had just been discharged.

Standing in the living room, Jack swung around to peer at his daughter, not quite knowing what to expect.

He had gotten in from the office less than half an hour ago and had been surprised to discover that no one was home yet. The silence was deafening and he found himself feeling restless. For more than one reason. Restless because he was accustomed to the feeling that his children were somewhere in the house, sleeping or causing havoc, and there was an odd sort of comfort in that knowledge.

Restless, too, because of the evening that still lay ahead of him.

He wasn't really comfortable about this "adventure" he was embarking on.

Jack's social skills began and ended in his professional world, where there was a safety net in place and where whatever went on could touch him only so far and no further. He had control over his professional life. *Felt* in control.

On a personal level, however, a completely different set of boundaries and parameters came into play. He felt as if he was out in the open, exposed. He didn't like that feeling, and that was exactly what dating did to a man— it put him out in the clearing, away from any sort of protective covering. Like a buck at the height of deer hunting season.

If he'd had a choice, Jack knew he wouldn't be going through this.

But he didn't have a choice. Not really.

He needed to find some sort of outlet for these pent-up feelings or else something re-grettable could happen. Something that, once done, couldn't be undone or taken back.

But right now, for this small segment of

time, he focused his attention exclusively on his little girl, who was pirouetting in front of him.

Emily looked like a little doll, he thought, and yet there was a hint of the young woman who was to be.

He had no idea where that strange, unexpected ache in his heart came from.

"Who is this vision?"

He addressed his question regarding his daughter to the woman coming in behind her. Glancing up, he saw that Zooey was herding his son before her. Both of her wrists were adorned with a multitude of rope handles attached to several shopping bags.

"Here, let me help," Jack offered, trying to take the bags from her.

Since they were all looped together over her wrists, it wasn't as easy a matter as it sounded. Jack found himself entangled with the handles and Zooey before she could successfully uncouple herself from the shopping bags.

He shook his head as he finally succeeded. "What did you do, buy out the whole mall?"

"No, just whatever came in her size," Zooey answered breezily. "I'm kidding," she quickly added when she saw the expression on his face. Jack was taking her at her word. The man *had* to lighten up. Didn't humor have any place in his world?

Not her concern, she told herself. Shrugging out of her coat, she quickly removed Jackie's jacket before he could escape. He wiggled to and fro, then made a break for freedom the second his arms were free.

"Daddy, you're not looking," Emily cried, tugging on his sleeve.

Putting the shopping bags down by the sofa, Jack looked at his daughter and smiled. "That's because I'm blinded by your beauty."

Emily beamed from ear to ear. Again he thought that his little girl was blossoming right before his eyes. "Really, Daddy?"

"Really."

Jack raised his eyes toward Zooey once more, to find that she was watching for his reaction. He was grateful for what she'd done for his daughter. None of the other nannies he'd employed had ever taken such an interest in either of his children. They saw their positions as a job, nothing more. Zooey was different. She effortlessly meshed everything together, acting more like family than an employee.

He'd gotten lucky, finding her. "She looks very pretty."

"Zooey did my hair." Emily turned her head so that he could get a better view of her French braids. "Do you like it?"

"Very much. You look very grown up," he told her, knowing that was what she wanted to hear. And to an extent, it was true. The little girl who had been running around the house just yesterday seemed to have disappeared. He felt a pang. Jack squatted down to her level. "Don't grow up too fast, Emily."

"Just a year at a time, Daddy," she told him solemnly, as if this was a plan she had carefully laid out for herself.

Jack laughed and hugged her to him. The next moment, he heard a crash behind him. Turning, he saw that there were books scattered on the floor. It was obvious that Jackie felt too much attention was going to his sister, and he wanted some of it diverted to him. The little boy had sent several books flying off the built-in bookcase flanking the flagstone fireplace.

Zooey looked toward Jack. "I think someone's cranky."

Jack began to protest, then realized she

wasn't making a comment about his own disposition. "Oh, you mean Jackie."

"This time," she allowed.

She supposed that sounded a little edgy and sarcastic, but she wasn't feeling as charitable as she had at the mall. That had all been about Emily, and about the little girl forming a closer bond with Olivia. But now Zooey's mood had become a little testy. Because Jack was going out.

Telling herself she had no business reacting this way, that Jack was just her employer and nothing more, had no effect. Common sense and reason refused to penetrate the blanket of hurt that seemed to be wrapped around her.

"What do you want for dinner?" she asked as she replaced the books on the shelves. "Oh, I'm sorry, I forgot. You're going out with Rebecca tonight." She pushed the last book onto the shelf, then looked at him over her shoulder. "It is tonight, isn't it?"

She didn't quite carry off the innocent air she was attempting to project. She knew that because Jack frowned at her.

"Yes," he replied. She could have gone ice-skating on his tone of voice.

Allowing a sigh to escape, Zooey bit down on the inside of her cheek in an effort to think before she spoke. She really didn't want to say anything she was going to be sorry for. Sitting back on her heels, she couldn't help giving him the once-over. "Is that what you're wearing?"

He was wearing the dark gray suit he'd worn to the office that morning. Despite the fact that today was Saturday and there was hardly anyone there, he still hadn't dressed casually. Being one of the partners of a high profile law firm dictated that he always dress formally, at least to his way of thinking.

After glancing down at his suit, he looked back at Zooey. "Yes, why? What's wrong with it?"

"Nothing." And there wasn't. He looked good. Too good. "I was just curious, that's all." She glanced at her watch. "Shouldn't you be going?"

His eyes were steely. "Shouldn't you be minding the children and not me?"

Zooey rose to her feet and straightened her shoulders. For the life of him, he couldn't read her expression. Not a comforting thought for a man who made his living by juries.

"I never mind you, Jack," Zooey replied with a smile that was paper-thin. And then she turned away, looking at the little girl who was quietly observing all of this. "Emily, why don't we take your things into your room?" Zooey scooped up the shopping bags again.

Emily came alive, sunshine radiating from her small face. "Okay! Can I try them on again?"

Zooey laughed at the joyous enthusiasm. At least she'd been successful with part of her day, she thought. "Sure. But then we have to hang everything up," Zooey told her. "Cuts down on ironing."

Emily nodded solemnly, as if she was the recipient of another heretofore forgotten commandment.

"Me, too?" Jackie demanded, obviously not wanting to be left out of whatever it was that his sister was going to be doing.

"Sure, you, too. Grab a bag, sport," Zooey encouraged, then picked out one for him to carry that had only a blouse in it. With that, she led the way out of the room, Jack watching every step she took.

When she returned to the living room more than forty minutes later, leaving Emily to revel in her new finery, and having put Jackie down for a quick nap, Zooey really didn't expect to find Jack still in the house, much less in the living room, where she'd left him.

It was getting late and she was going to have to see about throwing together some kind of dinner for herself and the kids. Or at least for the kids. To a great extent, her appetite had seemed to evaporate.

Her lips pulled into a tight smile. "You're still here."

Jack shoved his hands into his pockets. He was actually supposed to be leaving. But a general reluctance to begin that phase of the evening held him in place. "Yes."

Zooey paused and quietly studied him for a long moment. "Cold feet?" she guessed.

He didn't care for that assessment. Especially since it was so close to the truth. "What makes you say that?"

She forced herself to bank down her attraction to him and just think of Jack Lever as someone she was friendly with. Someone who looked a little lost right now.

"By my calculation, Rebecca is the first woman you've gone out with since you lost your wife."

Her assessment was too close for his comfort. He found himself wishing that he hadn't allowed Bo to catch him at a weak moment and talk him into this date.

"Very observant. Maybe you should be a private investigator."

Zooey kept her face as expressionless as his. "Maybe." She began to head for the kitchen, then stopped and turned toward him again. God, but he looked ill at ease. It took some of the edge off this strange, hurt feeling that kept assaulting her. "Would you like some advice?"

Knowing that he might not like what she had to say, he still said, "All right," because he was curious.

"Just be yourself and everything will be fine." It was the gold standard, given to everyone who had ever faced a "first date." She had no idea why she was saying that to him, except that Jack did look uncomfortable and she had this damn capacity for empathy. There were times, such as now, when that capacity seemed to be at cross-purposes with what she would have liked to be happening.

He laughed shortly, shaking his head. "I'll try to keep that in mind."

He turned to leave, and she called after him, "Your collar's up."

Jack stopped and glanced at her over his

shoulder. Lost in thought, all he'd heard was the sound of her voice, not the words.

"What?"

Rather than repeat herself, Zooey crossed to him and took care of the problem herself, carefully smoothing down the upturned corner of his collar.

That brought her up close and personal to him. So close that she could feel his breath on her face. Could feel her pulse quickening from the contact.

Zooey meant to drop her hand to her side, but somehow, she couldn't quite seem to make herself do it. Everything around her seemed to stand still. It was like being in a living photograph, where the moment was forever frozen in time.

His eyes were on hers, holding her in place.

And then his lips were on hers, and everything inside of her sighed, then exploded.

Except that it was more. Much more. More intense. More everything.

The hand that had refused to leave his collar now slipped along the back of his neck, joined there by her other hand.

Zooey leaned into the kiss and was thrilled to feel Jack's palms moving along her spine.

Drawing her to him. Her heart began to pound. Hard.

She felt the outline of his body against hers.

Her head began to swirl as the kiss deepened, growing until it blotted out everything else in the room. All thought, all time. Everything.

Zooey gave herself up to it, knowing she'd never felt anything close to the reaction she was having to Jack right this moment.

He had no idea what came over him.

One minute he was wrestling with his thoughts, with the stirrings he felt inside of him, trying to distance himself from everything. And the next moment, there was no distance at all. At least, not between him and this woman who somehow kept infiltrating his days, his life, his nervous system.

Jack gave in to the overwhelming curiosity that had dogged him even before he took her into his home. He had wondered what her lips would taste like ever since the day he'd watched them curve into a wide smile across the coffee shop counter.

They tasted the way he'd imagined—and felt soft, silky. They filled his senses, enflamed his blood.

He shouldn't be doing this. Shouldn't be giving in to curiosity and to desire and kissing his children's nanny. He was just minutes away from going out with another woman. Of course, the only reason he was going out with Rebecca Peters was so that he wouldn't be tempted to do exactly what he was doing right now....

"Daddy, are you kissing Zooey?"

The small, curious voice came out of nowhere and had them springing apart as if they'd been struck by lightening.

Out of the corner of his eye, Jack saw Zooey taking in several deep breaths. This kiss had left her just as breathless as it had him, he realized. There was a certain amount of satisfaction in that, but he was going to have to savor it some other time.

There was damage control to see to.

"Um, no. I'm not. I wasn't." Why was it that when he was in court, he could withstand the onslaught of even the most ruthless, well-seasoned lawyer, but the innocent question of a wisp of a girl could rattle him to his very bones? "Zooey had something in her eye and I was just trying to help get it out."

The expression on Emily's face told Jack

his daughter knew when she was being lied to. Her next words confirmed it.

"Daddies aren't supposed to fib, Daddy. You were kissing Zooey."

It was time to jump into the fray and save his butt, Zooey thought.

She put her hand on Emily's shoulder. The little girl looked up at her. "I was feeling sad, honey, and your daddy was just trying to make me feel better. You know, the way I kiss your hurt when you get one."

Emily's delicate eyebrows drew together in a perplexed blond line. "Why were you sad, Zooey?"

"Zooey no sad," Jackie declared, making his entrance by pushing his sister out of the way and rushing into the room.

And baby makes four, Zooey thought. Nap time had obviously been terminated. Jackie had more energy than any three children his age. If there was only some way to harness it.

Emily was still looking at her, waiting for an answer.

Zooey's mind raced, searching for something plausible to tell the little girl. And then she looked at the dress Emily was wearing. It was one they had picked out today.

"Because I didn't have time to get a whole bunch of pretty dresses, like you did."

Emily took her hand and wrapped her small fingers around it in a mute sign of comfort and camaraderie. "Next time," she promised solemnly.

Damn, how did some kids get to be so wonderful? Zooey could feel her heart overflowing with love. She wondered if Jack knew how very lucky he was. If she ever had a daughter, she hoped the girl would be half as sweet and generous as Emily was.

Using a laugh to cover the sudden desire to cry, Zooey hugged Emily to her. "Next time," she agreed.

Shaken to his roots by being caught in a compromising situation by his seven-year-old daughter, Jack restlessly ran a hand through his hair. That had been close. What if he'd allowed his control to slip even further? What if Emily had walked in on them not just kissing but— He couldn't allow his mind to go that route.

The way he saw it, he *needed* to go out with Rebecca more than he'd thought. Something had to cool his jets. Otherwise...

He didn't want to think about otherwise.

There were too many consequences if he went down that path.

He cleared his throat. When Zooey looked in his direction, he murmured, "I'd better be going."

She was still on her knees, hugging Emily.

"Yes, you'd better go." On a scale of one to ten, there was a minus-two level of enthusiasm in her voice. And then she forced a smile to her lips as she rose to her feet. "We'll keep a candle burning in the window for you," she joked. She saw Emily raise her head to stare at her, a quizzical expression on her face. "So you find your way home," Zooey concluded.

That's just the trouble. I know my way home. All too well. "Thanks," he said without emotion. And then he looked at his children, clustered around Zooey as if she were the center of their life.

She's just the nanny, nothing more, he insisted silently. "You two be good and listen to Zooey."

"Yes, Daddy," Emily said dutifully. Jackie made some kind of animal noise. Jack had no time to press for more of an answer; he was already late.

Emily turned away from the door the moment her father closed it and looked at Zooey. "Is Daddy going to get lost?" she asked.

Zooey knew she'd picked up on the candle in the window reference. Nothing got by this girl, she thought. "Let's hope not, Emily. Let's hope not." Then she took her hand. "C'mon, you can help me whip up something for dinner."

"Can we have mashed potatoes?" Emily asked.

"Just mashed potatoes?" Her brother Ethan had had an attachment to peas when he was a little boy. Just peas. Platefuls of peas for lunch and dinner. The phase had lasted almost four months.

"Gravy?" Emily added hopefully.

"Mashed potatoes and gravy it is," Zooey agreed. Luckily, she'd bought a bag of potatoes at the grocery store the other day.

Emily smiled broadly. She was a very picky eater, but the little girl loved mashed potatoes. Whatever worked, Zooey thought, desperately trying not to think about Jack and the woman three doors down.

What she had was a crush, Zooey insisted, nothing more. Women got them all the time and they usually lasted about as long as they sounded they would. Ten minutes. Twenty, tops. She'd be over him by morning.

But the imprint on her lips was not going to fade away by morning, she feared. Neither would the imprint on her soul.

It would if she ignored it, Zooey promised herself.

Just as Emily began to walk into the kitchen, she turned on her heel and beckoned for Zooey to bend down. When she did, Emily threw her arms around her and hugged her. Hard.

"Not that I didn't like that, Emily, but what's it for?" she asked once Emily's little arms had slipped from about her neck.

"You looked like you were being sad again," Emily told her simply.

That's because I was, Zooey thought. "I'm going to work on being happy," she vowed. And then she put her arm around Zooey's shoulders. "Unless, of course, I want another hug from you."

"You can have one, they're free," Emily assured her. And then the little girl looked at her for a long moment, as if she was trying to work something out in her head. "Zooey?"

"Yes?"

"Will you be my mommy?"

If she'd been eating or drinking anything at the moment, Zooey felt certain she would have begun to choke.

"Mommy, Mommy," Jackie repeated in a singsong voice. Zooey vaguely realized that the little boy had never called anyone by that name.

Mostly, though, she was stunned by Emily's question. That made twice in one week that she'd found herself at a loss for words.

She hoped this wouldn't get to be a habit.

Chapter Eight

When she could finally move her lips and engage part of her brain, Zooey asked the little girl, "What did you say?"

Emily repeated, "Will you be my mommy?" in the same tone of voice she'd used the first time.

Listening closer, Zooey realized that what Emily had said wasn't a request. She wasn't *asking* her to be her mother. It was a question regarding the chain of events that might take place, as in "Will you be my teacher next year?"

Still, where had this come from?

"Why would you ask me that, Emily?" she

inquired softly, not wanting Emily to think she was upset or rattled by the question.

It was apparently all very logical to her. "Because Daddy was kissing you. And you were kissing Daddy."

This girl was definitely going to go far, Zooey decided. If Emily was this observant now, there was no telling how astute and aware of things she was going to be when she grew up. Emily was also bright enough to disregard the excuse Zooey had given earlier about Jack attempting to cheer her up. There was no pulling the wool over this kid's eyes.

"Mommies and daddies kiss," Emily was saying, driving her point home. "I see it in the school yard sometimes."

For just the tiniest moment, Zooey entertained the idea. What would it be like, being Emily's mother? There were times when she felt she was more than halfway there. All that was missing from the picture was Emily's father.

Zooey's mouth curved. Not exactly a small point. "*People* kiss, Emily. If they like each other and the moment is right, they kiss."

Emily was very receptive to that explanation. It just helped to further her own version of things. "Is that what happened?" she demanded eagerly. "Do you like my daddy?"

Uh-oh. Quicksand dead ahead. Zooey deliberately chose an evasive way out. "Your daddy's a very nice man, Emily."

She was not about to be put off with vague answers. "Does my daddy like you?"

If that kiss is any indication of the way he feels, then yes, he likes me.

Again, Zooey remained nebulous. "He thinks I'm a good nanny." Opening the pantry, she took out the sack of potatoes and placed it on the counter before undoing the tie at the top.

Emily's small face scrunched up as she debated the merits of that endorsement. For now, she appeared to settle for what she could get. At least this meant Zooey would get to stay.

"Good. Because he didn't like the other nannies and they went away." She lowered her voice, like one adult confiding in another, and kept her eyes on her brother to make sure he wasn't listening. "I didn't like the other nannies, either. But I like you."

Moved, Zooey hugged Emily to her with one hand, while counting out potatoes on the counter with the other. "And I like you." She paused to kiss the top of Emily's head. "A lot."

"Me, too?" Jackie abandoned the truck he'd been making sound effects for, and wiggled in between them.

Annoyed, Emily began to push her brother away. Zooey stopped counting potatoes and knelt down between the two warring siblings, separating them and draping an arm around each child. She hugged them to her and tried hard not to notice the maternal stirrings that insisted on rising up within her.

"Yes, Jackie, you, too. I like both of you." She listened to herself. Since when had she been this careful? "I love both of you," she exclaimed.

With a small cry, Emily threw her arms around her, hugging her hard.

It was one of those nights when sleep absolutely refused to come or even make a token appearance.

Ordinarily, Zooey only had to get ready for bed and then crawl into it. Once there, she'd close her eyes and within seconds be dead to the world.

The last time she'd tossed and turned this much she'd been searching for the right way to tell her parents that she was dropping out of school. Dropping out of their plans for what amounted to the rest of her life.

Sighing, Zooey stared up at the ceiling and thought about today and how well things had gone.

Up to a point.

The shopping trip had turned out to be even better than she'd hoped. Emily and Olivia had bonded in that special little-girls-discovering-fashion-and-their-budding-power sort of way. The two really liked one another.

And Zooey and Megan had had a good time as well. Before today, she'd only exchanged a few words with Olivia's aunt. She'd discovered that Megan was a very nice person, not at all like some of the rumors claimed—that she was a home wrecker and worse. The woman was fun, loved her niece and was easy to talk to. It seemed as if Emily hadn't been the only one who had made a new friend today.

The personal highlight of Zooey's day, of course, had been the stop she'd made at her parents' house before the shopping trip began. She hadn't really looked forward to that. In fact, she'd been dreading it. She and her father hadn't exchanged a single word since she'd dropped out of college. She was sure today would only be more of the same.

She was wrong.

Oh, there'd been a frosted moment or two when her mother had ushered her into her father's workshop, and the two of them had just stood there, looking at each other. Two statues with pulses.

But all she'd had to say was, "Dad," and suddenly, he was there, hugging her and saying it was all right.

It was as if the silence of the last year and a half had never existed.

Zooey smiled to herself now. All that was good. But none of those things, separately or together, would have kept her awake like this.

It was waiting for Jack to come home that was doing that.

Waiting to hear his key in the lock, to hear the door opening and then closing again, telling her that he had come home. Alone.

Oh, God, what if he didn't come home alone? What if he brought *her* with him?

Or what if he'd decided to spend the night, or a good portion of it, at Rebecca's house? Zooey sincerely doubted that they'd spend the entire night quietly sipping tea and discussing lawn fertilizer. Rebecca was much too much woman for that.

Well, what was *she?* Zooey wondered. Chopped liver? He'd kissed her for God's sake. In front of his children, or at least in front of his daughter. Not that he'd planned it, but that was the way it had turned out. Didn't that mean anything?

Zooey pressed her lips together. Sure, it meant something. It meant Jack was using her to warm up for the main event.

Turning over on her belly, she dragged the pillow over her head in frustration. Damn it, she needed to get to sleep. She was going to be a wreck tomorrow. She had to stop driving herself crazy like this.

There was nothing between her and Jack except her wishful thinking. End of story.

Exasperated, Zooey sat up, throwing her pillow on the floor. She'd given up the larger room downstairs that Jack had initially told her was hers for a smaller one on the second floor. She'd wanted to be closer to Emily and Jackie so that she could hear them if they needed her during the night.

That left her straining to hear sounds that could have been coming from downstairs.

This was pathetic.

She needed a book, she decided, something to *put* her to sleep, since she couldn't seem to get there on her own power. Kicking the covers aside, she got up. The wooden floor felt cold against her feet. Zooey wiggled her toes into slippers, tugged on the robe she normally kept at the foot of the bed, and made her way downstairs.

She didn't bother tying the robe. Her mind wasn't on details. It felt restless and disoriented. Like the rest of her.

No sooner had she reached the bottom of the stairs than she heard the front door being unlocked. For a split second, she thought of running back up, but no matter how fast she moved, she knew that Jack would see her the moment the door opened.

The alternative was to make a mad dash for the shelter of the kitchen, but that seemed cowardly to her. So Zooey remained exactly where she was, her hand tightly wrapped around the banister, half expecting to see Rebecca walking in with Jack, most likely hanging on his arm or half draped along his body.

When he came in alone, Zooey's heart began to beat again.

Yes!

Lost in thought, thinking how he had done

smarter things in his time than what he'd done tonight, Jack didn't realize he wasn't alone when he first walked in.

He wasn't sure exactly what it was that caught his attention, but he looked up. And saw Zooey standing at the foot of the stairs. She was wearing a football jersey that should have been at least six inches longer, and a robe that should have been closed. For his sake if not for hers.

Now there was irony for you. Rebecca had worn a dress that almost wasn't there. And what there had been of it was as skintight as the laws of physics would allow. And yet seeing her like that hadn't aroused him half as much as seeing Zooey in her damn football jersey, with her damn robe hanging open, offering no protection, no barrier.

His mouth felt dry, as if he'd had an entire cup of sand to drink. He pocketed his key, attempting to distance himself from his thoughts, his reactions. He succeeded only marginally.

"What are you still doing up? Something wrong?" He cleared his throat to keep from croaking.

She shook her head. Movement was easy. Talking, or at least making sense, was the hard part. He wasn't home early, but at least he was home. Without *her*. "I just came down looking for a book."

"A book?" He glanced over her head up the stairs, listening for the sound of one of his children calling or fussing. He heard nothing. "To read to the kids?"

"To read to me," she told him with a smile. Had the date gone badly? God, she hoped so. "I couldn't sleep." But even as she tendered her excuse, Zooey found herself stifling a yawn. Chagrined, she flashed a quick, embarrassed smile. "I guess maybe I'm more tired than I thought I was."

She knew she should either go get a book or turn around and head back upstairs. She did neither. Clearing her throat, Zooey crossed to him, her hands buried deep in the pockets of her robe. "So," she began, trying to sound cheerful, "how was your date?"

Now here was something he wasn't prepared for—being quizzed by his children's nanny about his evening out. "You know, I'd ask you if you were my mother—except that my mother never asked questions like that."

Zooey laughed softly. Memories, embarrassing ones, came flying back to her from all sides. "Lucky you. My mother *always* asked questions like that. No matter what time I got in."

She'd once gotten in at four in the morning, only to find her mother still waiting up. The woman had incredible tenacity. The last Zooey had heard from Kim, their mom was still at it.

"Not so lucky," he commented, surprising her. Was that a sad note in his voice? "At least your mother cared."

Zooey knew she had no right to ask, to probe, but it wasn't in her nature to back away. It never had been. "Yours didn't?"

He slid the topcoat off, draping it on the coatrack, and shrugged in response to her question. "Not that I ever noticed."

Mothers cared, she thought. Most mothers cared too much, getting in their sons' way. "Maybe she just wanted you to think she didn't, while trying to give you your space."

He'd had space, all right. A whole continent of it. "She did that. Gave me my space from across the ocean." He saw Zooey looking at him oddly, as if he'd lost her. "Most of my high school years, my mother was away 'touring' Europe."

There was a cynical expression on his face, Zooey noted. If she scraped the surface, she was certain she'd find anger. "As in performing?"

He laughed at her question, but there was no real humor in the sound. "Who knows? Maybe." His mother liked to associate with famous people, people with bloodlines and pedigrees. Maybe she'd slept with a few, as well. "But the official version was that she was 'vacationing.' My stepfather was away so much, I don't know if he ever realized she wasn't around."

That sounded absolutely awful to Zooey. But she kept her pity under wraps, knowing he wouldn't appreciate it. "Not much of a home life."

She led the way to the kitchen. Because they were talking, Jack followed automatically. He shrugged in response to her comment. "The servants were cool. Sometimes."

Taking the pot from the coffeemaker, she poured water into it and transferred that into the urn. She didn't bother with the filter or coffee; she was going to make him some herbal tea. He looked as if he needed to be soothed.

"So that's where you get it from," she murmured. That explained a lot.

Jack lowered his frame onto a stool at the

counter, watching her. Watching the way the open robe moved and caught, allowing the outline of her body to take his imagination hostage.

"Get what from?" he demanded. "Zooey, what are you talking about?"

The coffeemaker began to make crackling, hissing sounds as the water found its way through the machine, heating in the process.

"You're imitating a pattern. The only one you've ever known. Your stepfather was a workaholic, so now you are, too."

Jack looked at her, annoyed, a stinging protest rising to his lips. But the words never emerged, because he realized she was right. Even though he'd hated his adolescent years, he was reliving them from the other side— doing the same thing to his children that his own parents had done to him. Getting lost in his own world, while mouthing platitudes that this was all for them. That he was working all these long hours for them.

It was himself he was doing it for. To feel worthwhile. To feel as if he was in control of some small part of his life.

Blowing out a breath, Jack ran a hand through his hair. He didn't like the fact that

she was right. But that didn't change anything.

He eyed Zooey as she reached up to get
cups from the cabinet. Her short jersey rode
higher, lighting a fire within him. He looked
away, trying to maintain some semblance of
decorum.

"What was it you said your degree was in?"
he murmured.

"I didn't." Placing a tea bag in each cup,
she took the pot and poured hot water into
both. "And I don't have a degree," she corrected. "I dropped out during the last semes-
ter before graduation."

He winced as if he'd just received a physical blow. He knew how he would have felt if
Emily pulled that kind of stunt on him. "I'll
bet that didn't go over very well at home."

He had the gift of understatement, she
thought, setting the pot back on the burner.
"That would be a bet you'd win."

Curiosity got the better of him. "Why did
you drop out?"

Ah, the million dollar question. Too bad
she didn't have a million dollar answer. Just
a whole bunch of little ones that didn't seem
all that good when she said them out loud.

"Because I could," she told him. "Because I

didn't want to be dictated to, even by my family. Especially by my family," she amended, remembering the period she'd been through. "Because I didn't want to 'conform.' And maybe," she concluded quietly, "because I was scared."

"Scared?" He said the word, but it really wasn't registering. Jack couldn't picture Zooey being afraid of anything. She struck him as being absolutely fearless, even when common sense would dictate caution. "You?" he scoffed. "Of what?"

She set his cup of tea before him, knowing he didn't care for cream or sugar. As far as she was concerned, the more cream and sugar, the better.

"Of what was expected of me once I had that degree," she told him, saying something she hadn't even admitted to herself until this moment. "If I didn't have the degree, they couldn't expect me to be like them. Perfect."

"So, if I'm following you correctly, in order not to disappoint your parents, you decided to disappoint them big time."

He made it sound stupid. Hell, maybe it was at that, she thought.

Zooey grinned with a dismissive shrug. "I

don't exactly do my best work when I'm feeling desperate."

He was still thinking about the unfinished degree. It seemed a shame to put in so much work, only to walk away from the finish line a second before the race was over. He took a sip of tea, his eyes never leaving her face. "Why don't you go back and finish up? Get your degree," he coaxed. "You know what they say. A mind is a terrible thing to waste."

"Maybe," she allowed. "But as far as my going back to finish up my degree, I can't. You see, I have this job I like, and the guy, he kind of depends on me to be there for his kids."

Jack laughed. He hadn't forgotten about that part. It wasn't as if he wanted her to leave. "There are always evening classes."

"The kids are there in the evenings, too," she said with a perfectly straight face.

His deadpan expression faded before hers did. "Yes, but the 'guy' could be, too."

Her eyes met his. This was new, she thought. Usually she had to beg him to put in an appearance once a night in the children's rooms. "That would mean he'd have to make an effort to come home earlier."

Jack stopped being so vague. "I could make

it home earlier than I have been." He gazed into her eyes, even as he told himself to stop doing that. "For a worthy cause."

It was a struggle not to feel flattered. Zooey knew he didn't mean it that way, but she still felt warm. And touched. "What about your cases?"

He laughed. The woman certainly did know how to throw up obstacles. "Ever hear about bringing your work home with you?"

She'd heard of it, but hadn't expected him to do it. Not when he hadn't before. She wondered if something was up, and told herself to stop being so suspicious.

Sliding her cup beside his, she settled on the stool next to his. "You'd do that? For me?"

God, but Zooey's eyes were wide. And beautiful. He'd never noticed that before. It was difficult trying to focus on the conversation. Hard fending off this urge that had only gotten stronger since his date with Rebecca.

"You had a good point. I should be spending more time with the kids," he agreed. "And if I *am* home, there's no reason why you couldn't take a few classes until you satisfy your degree requirements."

She laughed, shaking her head. This had to be the *last* thing she'd ever expected to hear from him. "My mother would really like you. She's already crazy about Jackie," she added. Instead of being worn-out, her mother had been reluctant to give the boy up at the end of the day.

Jack was looking at her quizzically, waiting for clarification. "I left Jackie with her today when I took Emily and Olivia shopping."

He nodded. He'd almost forgotten about the shopping spree. He took a sip of the tea she'd prepared for him, but it was going to take more than herbal tea to quell what was going on inside of him. Still, he appreciated the effort, even if he couldn't say so out loud. "Emily seemed a lot happier than I've seen her in a long time."

She was very pleased with herself for that, she decided. "Well, she's got a new best friend and a new wardrobe. At seven, her world is just about perfect."

"Thank you." The words came out of nowhere.

Zooey tried to second-guess what he was talking about. "For the tea?"

He shook his head. "For my daughter's happiness." He moved the cup away and studied her. "You're really a very special person, Zooey."

Compliments embarrassed her. She never knew what to say. Declaring, "No, I'm not," didn't quite seem the way to go here. Still, the situation begged for something. "Your kids make it easy."

Which just made her that much more unique in his book, Jack thought.

"Not to hear the other nannies talk about it. They thought the kids were hell on wheels. Of course, they weren't very thrilled with me, either. Said I was too demanding. And 'too invisible,'" he said, quoting one of the women. "Whatever that means."

Zooey leaned her chin in her hand, gazing at him. "You look pretty visible to me." Then she stopped. Taking a napkin out of the holder on the counter, she draped it over her index finger and wiped it along the corner of his mouth. When he pulled his head back, she said, "Pink isn't your color," and held up the corner of the napkin with traces of lipstick on it.

He cleared his throat. "Rebecca kissed me."

"Well, I didn't think she tried to brand you with it."

Zooey was sitting too close. And his resolve was only so strong. He wasn't going to be able to resist her much longer. Wasn't going to keep his curiosity about what she looked like beneath that jersey under lock and key more than a couple more minutes.

Squaring his shoulders, he stood up. "I'm going to turn in," he said abruptly.

"I'll stay down here and clean up," she murmured, more to herself than to him.

She sighed as she heard him go up the stairs. For every step she took forward, there was another step back, waiting to be taken.

And in the end, she was standing in the same place where she'd begun. And damn confused about how she got there.

Chapter Nine

Zooey closed the front door behind her. She'd just ushered her charges into the house after picking up Emily and Olivia at school and dropping the latter at her house.

There was homework to get to and dinner to start, but Zooey firmly believed in balancing out work with play. She had milk and chocolate chip cookies waiting for the children in the kitchen. Leaving the treats out without having Jackie get into them had been the tricky part.

Under Zooey's watchful eye, both children took their turn at getting up on the wooden step she had butted up against the sink and washing their hands before sitting down at the table.

Zooey paused to wipe the area around the sink after Jackie had finished. There was enough water there to fill half a duck pond.

"Are you excited about Halloween?" Zooey asked Emily as she hung up the towel again.

"Halloween, Halloween," Jackie cried, providing the excitement that was missing from Emily's face.

He was like a three-foot-tall tape recorder, repeating everything he heard, Zooey thought. But the little boy wasn't her main concern at the moment. Emily was. Granted, Zooey had gotten the child started. Once or twice in the last few weeks she'd even heard Emily begin a conversation when she was around Olivia. But she needed more. Something to give her more confidence, make her feel as if she blended in better.

The displays of Halloween candy in the supermarket—the displays Jackie had made a beeline for before she managed to grab him—had given her an idea. Emily could have a Halloween party, one for the children in the neighborhood and their parents. It wouldn't hurt Jack to do a little mingling, either—with someone other than Rebecca.

Getting permission for the party was going to require some finessing on Zooey's part when it came to Jack. But before she undertook that, she needed to get Emily on board. If the little girl regarded the holiday in the same manner that most kids regarded broccoli, there was no point in knocking herself out.

Still, she couldn't picture any child not liking Halloween.

"Maybe," Emily finally said. The single word was accompanied by a vague, careless shrug of her small shoulders.

When Zooey and her siblings had been little, they couldn't wait for Halloween to come around. To them, it was almost as big a holiday as Christmas. She didn't understand Emily's lack of enthusiasm.

She sat down at the table, taking a cookie. There was already a circle of crumbs around Jackie's plate, along with splotches of milk. She was letting him sit on a booster seat instead of his high chair today, and was beginning to doubt the wisdom of that move.

"Don't you like dressing up for Halloween, going trick-or-treating?" Zooey pressed.

Emily looked at her for a long moment as

if she was talking about something entirely foreign. "We don't go trick-or-treating."

This might be easier to pull together than she'd thought. "Because you have a party?" Zooey asked.

Emily shook her head. "No."

And then again, maybe not. "Do you dress up?" Again, Emily shook her head. "Why not?"

Emily sighed, and it was clear to Zooey that it was a wistful sound. "The last two nannies we had said it was silly."

How had Jack managed to find such heartless creatures? What kind of an ad had he put out? "Wanted: one nanny, completely devoid of a sense of humor or any memories of childhood."

Zooey dunked her cookie in milk and held it out to Emily. "You're a kid. You're supposed to be silly. And anyway, dressing up for Halloween isn't silly," she said defensively. "It's a tradition. It's fun."

Emily now appeared to be hanging on every word. Her eyes were wide. Hopeful. "Do you dress up on Halloween, Zooey?"

"Absolutely." She leaned closer to the girl. "How would you like to have a Halloween party this year?"

If eyes could truly sparkle, then Emily's did. "A real party?"

Zooey grinned broadly. "A real party."

There was awed disbelief on Emily's small, heart-shaped face. "With balloons and everything?"

"With balloons and everything," Zooey echoed, making a note to find the biggest, prettiest balloons she could. She didn't believe in scary Halloweens, but ones filled with princesses and unicorns and everything magical.

And then suddenly, the enthusiasm that had been building in Emily's voice all but vanished. As did the light from her face. "Daddy won't like it."

"You leave your daddy to me," Zooey told her. "He's going to love it."

Emily obviously still had her doubts, but it was also obvious that she thought Zooey could walk on water and work miracles whenever she needed to. "You think?"

"I think." It was more than a statement, it was a promise.

Emily jumped up from the table and threw her arms around her. Her heart bursting, Zooey hugged the girl fervently.

"You're the best, Zooey."

"Yes, I am," she laughed, squeezing Emily a little harder. And praying that the man she'd hardly seen in the last week—ever since his so-called date with the neighborhood vixen—could be convinced to come around.

"Best!" Jackie crowed, scrambling off his chair and sending the booster seat flying as he tried to claim his share of his nanny.

Zooey's heart stopped for half a second as she grabbed him in time to keep him from crashing to the floor.

"You are going to be the death of me, boy," she told him.

"Death!" he yelled.

"But not before the Halloween party," she added, looking at Emily.

"Not even after," Emily said fervently.

There was no stopping the warm feeling once it took hold. Zooey wrapped her arms around the children and hugged them hard.

That night she waited up for Jack to ask him about the party. Loaded for bear, she intended to give him both barrels if necessary, use every trick she could think of to get him to agree, including guilt.

So, after she had put Emily and Jackie down for the night and made sure they'd fallen asleep, she went back to the living room and planted herself in the oversize chair that faced the doorway. It was extremely seductive in its comfort.

Zooey sighed as she sank into it. She'd put in a long day with the children. Teachers were giving second graders a lot more homework these days than they had when she was Emily's age, she thought grudgingly. Emily was very bright, but Zooey wasn't about to fluff off the job of checking the little girl's work by just assuming everything was correct— which, of course, it had been.

The next moment, Zooey found herself wondering if Jack would soon be married to someone else who would help Emily with her homework.

The thought brought a pang with it, a sharp one that went straight to Zooey's heart even as she struggled to dismiss it. It wasn't supposed to matter to her whom the man married, whom he finally selected to act as a mother to his children.

It wasn't supposed to, but it did, she admitted with another sigh as she checked her watch. It was getting late.

She had Jack's dinner prepared, covered and waiting for him in the warming oven. By her count, it had been there for several hours.

Didn't the man remember his way home anymore?

That was the last thought that passed through her head before she nodded off to sleep.

The sound of the front door closing had Zooey jerking her head up. Blinking, she automatically looked down at her watch. It was a habit, a holdover from her college days, when she'd had a tendency to oversleep and miss her early classes.

She'd been asleep for almost an hour. Grabbing the armrests, Zooey pushed herself up out of the chair. A second later, she realized that she'd gotten up too fast. A wave of dizziness, something that plagued her occasionally whenever she forgot to eat right, had her head spinning. She swayed just as Jack was entering the room.

"Zooey, what's the matter?"

She felt his arms close around her, catching her before she could sink back down to the chair. His voice held a note of concern. Forcing herself to focus, she took a deep breath, then let it out again.

"Nothing. I fell asleep in the chair and got up too fast," she explained simply.

Jack searched her face to assure himself

there wasn't more going on that she wasn't mentioning. Her color began to return.

"What are you doing up?" he asked. He'd deliberately come home at this hour to avoid seeing her. The last thing he'd expected was to have to rush forward and catch her in his arms before she fell. "It's late. You should be in bed."

She took another breath. It was hard to get her bearings when he was this close to her. "That's what you're supposed to say to your daughter, not me."

"She's not up," he pointed out. "You are." Jack realized that he was still holding her. And that he liked it far too much. "Can I let go of you? Can you stand on your own?"

"Yes and yes."

He dropped his hands, and something inside of her felt bereft.

"As for what I'm doing up, I'm waiting for you to come home."

Concern returned, driving a chariot straight into the arena. He looked toward the stairs and the children's bedrooms. "Is something wrong?"

Turning back, he watched her work her lower lip between her teeth. "Only if you say no."

Clear as mud. His day had been long and his nerve endings were raw. That didn't leave a lot of room for patience. "I know why the kids like you so much. You talk in riddles."

Zooey needed him to be in a receptive mood. A full stomach helped. She backtracked. "There's dinner in the warming oven."

"I ate."

She looked at him, not ready to give up. "What?"

"I ate," he repeated.

Zooey shook her head. "No, not what did you say, what did you eat?"

He thought for a moment. He could remember chewing, but nothing had actually registered on his palate.

"I'm not sure," he admitted. "Some chickeny thing one of the law clerks brought in from a fast food place."

There had been three of them staying late, working on their individual cases. When the intern had volunteered to make a food run, Jack had given him a ten, but no instructions beyond getting something that wasn't too greasy. He vaguely recalled being told they were chicken strips. Fries had come with that, but he'd skipped them.

Jack started for the stairs, and was surprised when Zooey hooked her arm through his and tugged him in the direction of the kitchen.

Now what? "What are you doing?"

"Taking you to the kitchen for a real meal." She wasn't about to take no for an answer. "I made meat loaf. The kids loved it."

He frowned as he crossed the threshold into the kitchen. The lights were all on. Instead of appearing lonely, the room seemed welcoming. He was overtired, he decided.

"I don't like meat loaf."

Zooey picked up two pot holders. "You'll like this one."

He didn't seem to have a say in anything anymore. What was worse, he was too tired to be annoyed about it. "Anyone ever tell you that you're damn pushy?"

She looked at him over her shoulder, her mouth curving. "I might have heard a rumor to that effect. You'll like the meat loaf," she repeated, taking a plate out of the oven. "Honest." She closed the stove door with one swift movement of her hip, then brought the plate to the table. "It has carrots, two kinds of peppers, onions, scallions and sour cream in it, not to mention a whole bunch of other things. It's a meal all by itself."

He had to admit that it did smell tempting.

But then, so did she. Despite her rapid-fire delivery, there were still traces of sleepiness around Zooey's eyes, and he found that exceedingly sexy for some reason. He had another date set with Rebecca, their third, but that didn't take the edge off the way he was reacting to Zooey. It should have, but it didn't. Just as he'd been afraid it wouldn't.

He'd kept away from the house, from her, for most of the last ten days, and that still didn't negate or even blunt the attraction he felt toward her. If anything, it sharpened it. Zooey intrigued him, amused him, attracted him.

Any way he sliced it, Jack felt doomed.

And there wasn't a damn thing he could do about it, because he needed a nanny and the kids were wild about her. And she seemed to be the only one who could keep them from being wild, period.

Doomed.

"Here, try some." Zooey moved the plate closer to him and handed him a fork. "Sit," she instructed, when he still remained standing.

He did as she asked, his knees bending mechanically until he made contact with the chair. Under her watchful eye, he sank his fork into the meat loaf, corralled a piece and brought it to his lips. He fully expected not to taste anything at all, because his mind was definitely not on food at the moment.

But the moist, flavorful forkful managed to break through the barriers around him. Surprised, he took another sampling. And then another. It tasted better each time.

"Well?" she asked when he said nothing. That he was eating it was certainly testimony that he liked it, but she wanted him to say the words. The man needed to express himself, so that he could verbalize his feelings to his children, who needed to hear them a lot more than she needed to be complimented on her cooking. But a start had to be made somewhere.

"Not bad," he murmured.

"Not bad?" she echoed. If he'd been one of her brothers, he would have been on the receiving end of a head-rattling shove. Curbing the impulse, she demanded, "Did they repossess your taste buds, too?"

He laughed then, at her expression, at her choice of words and at her exasperation over his so-called indifference to what he had to admit was probably the best meal he'd had in a while. Which was saying a lot, seeing as how she'd been doing all the cooking since January.

"This is good," he admitted.

Damn straight it's good. She waved for him to keep moving his fork. "Eat up," she told him. "There's plenty more where that came from."

"So what is it that you want to talk to me about?" he asked after three more forkfuls had found their way into his mouth.

Sitting down again, Zooey took a deep breath, bracing herself for an argument. Knowing she needed to win it. "I thought you might have a party for Emily."

"A party?" he echoed in surprise. "Why? It's not her birthday." And then he paused for a second, trying to remember what month it was. "Is it?"

Zooey stared at him, stunned. Just how wrapped up in his work was he? "You don't know when your daughter's birthday is?"

"Of course I do." He was annoyed that she could even suggest such a thing. "It's June. June 11th. Working late, I just lose track of time sometimes," he admitted. "The weeks and months get jumbled up." This wasn't the first time he'd had to stop to get his bearings, unable to recall what month it was.

"Dusty books will do that to you." Not wanting to alienate him, she turned to the business at hand. "I'm talking about a Halloween party," Zooey specified. "I think you need to throw a Halloween party for Emily."

"Need?" he echoed. The woman used the strangest words sometimes. What he *needed* was peace and quiet, neither of which seemed to be in his immediate future. "Zooey, I don't know the first thing about throwing a party."

She hadn't really meant that he was going to be the one in charge of it. That would have been a disaster waiting to happen. "Lucky for you, I do."

Finished with the meat loaf, he set down his fork and took another sip of water. "I never doubted it. But before you get carried away here, why do I 'need' to throw my daughter a Halloween party? I thought things were going well for her and Odette—"

"Olivia," Zooey corrected. "The girl's name is Olivia. And they are, but Emily needs to branch out a little more. She needs to learn how to have fun."

"That's why I have you." That did *not* come out the way he'd meant it, Jack thought, afraid that Zooey might take offense. "I mean, that's what you're supposed to provide for her."

"Which I'm trying to do," she emphasized, bringing the conversation back full circle. "As soon as you say yes to the party."

He was not the kind of man anyone ever accused of leaping first and looking later. Before he jumped into a pool, he not only looked it over but asked to review the building specs on it as well. Giving his permission for the party came under the same heading. He needed to have more input before he agreed. Who knew what Zooey thought constituted a party?

"Just how many people are you planning to invite to this so-called party?"

She could almost see the way his mind worked. "Not the immediate world," she assured him. "Just the kids in the neighborhood— and their parents."

Zooey had her mind made up, he could see that. He could also see why this would be good for Emily. He'd never had a party of his own when he was a kid, and maybe that was part of the reason that socializing without a legal brief in his hand had always been difficult for him. "When's Halloween?"

"Same day it's always been—October 31st. In two weeks," she added, in case today's date escaped him.

"Sure, go ahead." Pushing back his chair, he rose from the table. "I suppose I can stay late in the office even if I'm not on a case—"

"No, no, no!" Zooey interrupted with such feeling that Jack stopped in midsentence and stared at her. "You have to be here."

He saw absolutely no reason for his presence to be required. "Why?"

"Because it's for the *parents* as well," she emphasized, "and the last I looked, you're Emily's parent."

The thought of attending a party with a bunch of kids running around sent a shiver up his spine. Mingling with adults he didn't know all that well held no attraction for him, either.

"You can take my place."

"I don't look mean enough." The words were out of her mouth before she could stop them.

"Mean?"

He'd never thought of himself as being mean, especially not around the children. Granted, he wasn't around them all that much, but when he was, he never raised his voice, never lost his temper no matter how rambunctious Jackie became.

Zooey backpedaled tactfully. "Okay, maybe

stern is a better word. You do scowl a great deal," she pointed out. He looked surprised. Didn't he know? "Of course, you can do that on Halloween because it'll go with the costume."

This was getting out of hand very quickly. "What costume?"

"The pirate costume you'll be wearing," she answered innocently.

The hell he was. Jack knew he had to lay down the law to Zooey very succinctly. "I will not be wearing a pirate costume."

"Oh?" She could easily envision him as a pirate. There was a hidden, rakish side to him. Otherwise, she wouldn't be so attracted to him. But she wasn't going to push that if he wanted to go another route. "Then what kind of costume do you want to wear? I've got to get to the stores soon to find one in your size. They run out fairly quickly."

She said that as if she was familiar with the supply and demand of Halloween costumes. He had no doubt that she probably was. "A jacket, matching trousers and a tie," he answered.

She should have known. Zooey shook her head. The man had to get with the program. "The object is to dress like something other than what you are. If we don't find a costume to your liking, I can sew one."

That caught him off guard. "You sew?"

She knew she didn't look like the domestic type. Yet she loved to cook, loved caring for children, she'd discovered. And sewing relaxed her, she'd told him.

She did *not* strike him as a relaxed woman. "You haven't sewn much lately, have you?"

She laughed. "That's the first time I've heard you make a joke."

"I wasn't joking." It was merely an observation on his part. "Look, Zooey, you can do whatever you think is necessary to make my daughter happy. I'll give you my credit card and you can get anything you want for this party—"

"Good, because the first thing I want is you." That came out a little too quickly, with a little too much feeling, she thought. "For Emily," she added. "How do you think she'll feel when all the other kids have their parents there and she's the only one without a mother or father in attendance?"

He supposed she had a point, even though he hated to admit it. "You're an expert at this guilt thing."

Zooey laughed, taking his plate to the sink

and rinsing it before putting it in the dishwasher. "I had a great teacher."

"Your mother?" he guessed.

"My father." She closed the dishwasher door, then turned to face him. "So, you'll come?"

He really didn't want to, but she had his back against the wall. "You make it sound like Emily will spend the next ten years in therapy if I don't."

Then her work here, Zooey thought, was done. At least for the time being. Before turning off the light, she smiled at Jack. "I'm glad we understand each other."

Not hardly, he thought as he followed her out of the kitchen. He really doubted that he would ever understand the way her mind worked.

A pirate. He sighed inwardly. There had to be a way around that. He had two weeks to find it.

Chapter Ten

Caches of candy began showing up throughout the house in strange places. There were three bags on the top shelf above the built-in cabinets in his three-car garage. There were four hidden inside his bedroom closet, where even Jack couldn't reach them without first pressing a stepstool into service.

When he groped for a seldom-perused book on the uppermost shelf in his study and was unexpectedly showered with a hailstorm of M&M's that had torn loose from their bag, he figured it was time for an explanation.

It only took calling her name twice to get Zooey to put in a personal appearance.

"You bellowed, sir?" she asked, wiping her damp hands on her apron.

"I didn't bellow, I called," he informed her coolly. "Forcefully," he added when she gave him a penetrating look. "What's this?" He nodded at the floor.

Crossing the threshold, Zooey made her way to the scene of the crime. She looked down where he indicated and pretended to study the items in question earnestly. Then she looked up at him, a tranquil smile on her lips. "M&M's, I believe. Orange and black," she added.

"I know what they are," he muttered between gritted teeth. "What are they doing on my bookshelf? And in my garage? And behind the wineglasses in the kitchen? And God only knows where else." Exasperated, he paused. "Have you acquired some kind of a sugar fixation in the last few weeks that I should know about?"

Zooey didn't answer immediately. Instead, she smiled at him. He was familiar with that smile. It was the one she used with the children when she was patiently allowing them to prattle on until they tired themselves out. Ordinarily, he found it rather endearing.

Aimed at him, he found it irritating as hell.

"No," she finally replied as she bent down and began to gather up the scattered candy, depositing the pieces into her apron.

He found himself addressing the top of her head, a completely dissatisfying way to conduct an inquisition, in his opinion. "Then why are there stashes of candy all over the house?"

The fallen candy secure in the artificial fold of her apron, Zooey rose to her feet. "Halloween, Jack," she reminded him.

"Is a week away," he responded.

He knew that because he was keeping track of the date, despite all the other things he had on his mind. He was still trying to come up with a viable reason why he couldn't attend the party, or at least not attend it wearing some ridiculous costume. He'd never worn one as a kid and saw no reason to start now, at his age.

But for some reason, saying no didn't seem an option in this case.

Zooey looked at him as if she couldn't fathom his not comprehending her reasoning. "I don't like leaving things to the last minute. Most of the good candy is gone by then."

He blew out a breath, mystified. The woman came up with the oddest explanations. "I had no idea that there was good candy and bad candy."

When she raised her eyes to his, Jack could have sworn there was a hint of pity in them. He resented it, and squared his shoulders.

"Weren't you ever a kid?" she asked.

He didn't see what that had to do with it. "Yes, but I didn't spend my time grading candy."

She had a feeling that he'd never gone trick-or-treating as a kid, either. Otherwise, he'd know.

"Good candy," she explained patiently, "is the kind that all the kids are familiar with, the name brands. Bad candy is what the stores try to pass off at the tail end of a holiday like Halloween or Easter. It's cheap and tastes that way."

He wasn't about to argue with her, not over something so trivial. "If you say so." He sighed, looking at the ripped bag. "How much of this stuff do you have stashed around the house?"

"Not enough yet," she told him frankly. "But I'm getting there."

In his opinion, they had more than enough to rot the teeth of every kid in the neighborhood. "And you're hiding the bags because...?"

"I don't want to have to rush either of your children, especially Jackie, to the emergency room for a chocolate overdose," she answered patiently. "Or spend the day cleaning up after him when he throws up. In case you didn't know, your son absolutely cannot resist chocolate."

Actually, Jack didn't know that. He supposed there was a great deal he didn't know about his children that Zooey did. But then, she was with them more than he was.

"I see your point." About to say something else, he stopped. Zooey was reaching toward him. The next moment, her fingers were in his hair. "Zooey?"

She grinned as she held a small, round object up for him to see. "You had an orange M&M in your hair." Without thinking, she popped it into her mouth.

Why the hell he found that unnervingly sensual, he had no idea.

Maybe he was undergoing a brain meltdown, Jack thought. Whatever the reason, it took him a second to get his mind back into gear.

Clearing his throat, he nodded toward the doorway, hoping she would take the hint. He needed some space. "Okay, you've explained it. Sorry to take you away from whatever it was you were doing."

She wasn't moving, Jack noted. "Just washing dishes."

That didn't make any sense. "We have a dishwasher for that."

Zooey shook her head. "There aren't enough dirty dishes to make it worthwhile running it." It unsettled her sense of order.

Moving toward his wastebasket, she formed a funnel with her apron and sent the candy she'd gathered up raining into the container. Finished, she raised her eyes to his. "Have you given it any more thought?"

Jack gave up trying to ignore her so he could get back to perusing the textbook that had started all this in the first place. There *was* no ignoring Zooey, at least not when she was within a few feet of him. He sighed, putting the book down on his desk. "Given what any more thought?"

Zooey cocked her head and looked at him. She was wearing that tolerant smile again. "Your costume," she prompted.

He wondered what it took to get the word *no* across to this woman. "Yes, I've given it some more thought and the thought is no."

She shook her head, indicating that his

response was unacceptable. "What other thoughts have you had on the subject?"

He could feel his temper heating up. Why amusement seemed to be hovering at the same time, he had no clue. Being around Zooey always seemed to put him at cross-purposes.

But lines had to be drawn, boundaries had to be reestablished, since they had obviously gotten blurred. She was taking far too much upon herself. "That all the other nannies I've hired for my kids had enough sense not to bother me with trivia like this."

Zooey seemed unfazed by his words and his tone. "Well, too bad. They're gone, I'm not."

There was that amusement again, he noted, shaking his head. "You really don't have the proper employee mentality, you know that?"

She squared her shoulders, an indication that if he meant to put her in her place, he had failed. Miserably. "You're within your rights to fire me anytime you want, Jack."

He realized that she was sticking out her chin. Obviously a symbolic gesture, he thought, exasperated. "I don't want to fire you, Zooey."

"Good," she said, nodding her head. "Because I don't want to have to look for another job." And she didn't. For the first time since she'd left school, she really liked what she was doing. It wasn't just a way to pay the bills, but a way to make a difference in the lives she touched.

He seized his opportunity. "Keeping that in mind, maybe you could see your way to cutting me some slack on this."

She looked surprised that he could even say that. "I am. I haven't said anything to you about the costume for a whole week."

"And I appreciate it. Now if you could just continue that way…"

Her expression told him he was living in a fool's paradise even before she said anything to confirm it. "Sorry, can't. Time's getting short. Halloween is next Sunday, and like I said, you wait too long, there's nothing left to pick over."

She'd just made his point for him, he thought. "Exactly."

Zooey continued as if he hadn't said anything at all. "Seeing that you're so busy and in such demand, I decided to pick up a costume for you to try on." Then, just in case he thought he was stuck with it no matter what, she quickly added, "I know the guy who runs the shop and he said if this didn't fit, I could bring it back."

It was like watching a snowball descend down a hillside, gaining speed and girth. And waiting for it to swallow him up. Well, he had no intention of being swallowed up.

"Just exactly what part of 'I don't want to dress up' do you not understand?" he demanded.

"All of it," she answered cheerfully, as she exited the room.

Zooey was back in less than three minutes, holding a large box in her hands with the logo Fantasy written across it in big, bold red letters. When Jack made no move to take it from her, she thrust the box at him.

"Here. Try this on for fit," she urged. "I took my best guess, but I'm not all that good when it comes to sizing up men." There was amusement in her eyes as she said it.

Part of him wanted to stand firm, to tell Zooey that she probably knew damn well what she could do with the costume. But the part of him that had urged him to become a lawyer, that believed in order and prescribed ways of doing things, figured if he put the damn thing on and let her see how ludicrous he looked, she would finally leave him in peace.

Or so the theory went.

So he took the box from her and walked into the powder room down the hall to change, and finally put this verbal tug-of-war between them to rest once and for all.

Anticipation hummed through Zooey as she waited for Jack to return. It was, she supposed, like waiting to see if reality lived up to her fantasy. Since staying still was not something she had ever managed to do with aplomb, she began to straighten up the study, carefully stacking the books he'd left scattered all over on his desk.

It was rather ironic that she took better care of Jack's house than she ever did of the tiny apartment she'd lived in before moving here. She supposed that there was something about Jack and his children that brought her nesting instincts to the surface, that made her want to take care of the three of them, because, in different ways, they all needed to be taken care of.

It was an entirely new sensation for her, a new emotional grouping to reckon with.

And, if she moved fast enough, she didn't have any time left over to dwell on the fact that she had the same need within her. The need to lean on someone, to have someone who was willing to take over.

Not all the time, of course, but once in a while. When the burden on her shoulders grew too heavy. Even just the knowledge that there was someone willing to take over would have been enough.

She supposed that what it boiled down to was having someone to love. Someone who loved her back.

Zooey sighed.

She was getting maudlin. She was going to have to watch that. Being maudlin was ordinarily as foreign to her as shoes were to a duck.

The slight noise behind her had Zooey instantly turning toward the doorway. Since she'd moved into Jack's house, her reflexes had become razor sharp. They had to be. She never knew when Jackie might decide to take a dive from one of the bookcases.

For a second, her heart stopped.

Because her fantasy had taken on flesh and blood.

Humoring her, Jack had put on the entire costume, down to the shoulder-length wig and wide hat with its colorful scarlet plume.

He looks magnificent.

This wasn't a garden-variety cheap costume made to last a night before it began to fall apart. She had gone out of her way to find an exact duplication of what a well-heeled pirate might have worn three hundred years ago while plundering his way across the seven seas.

There was no doubt about it, Zooey thought. In another life, Jack Lever had been a swashbuckler. Every woman's fantasy come to life.

"Well?" he finally asked, when she made no comment. He was feeling progressively more stupid by the nanosecond.

Zooey swallowed, searching for saliva so that her lips wouldn't find themselves sealed together midword. Her mouth remained annoyingly dry. "You need a sword," she finally said.

Her comment seemed to come out of left field. "What?"

"A sword. To complete the outfit. You need a sword," she repeated. *And I definitely need oxygen before I make an idiot of myself.* As subtly as she could, Zooey drew in a lungful of air.

"If I had a sword, I might be tempted to use it." It was a warning. Holding his arms out at his sides, Jack turned around full circle until he was facing her again. Well, at least she wasn't laughing, he consoled himself. But she had to see how absurd he looked in this outfit. "Okay, say it."

Zooey looked at him, puzzled. "Say what?" *Uncle? Okay, I say uncle, or whatever it is someone says when they surrender.*

Because she did. She surrendered. Completely and utterly. She'd always thought that Jack was good-looking in a dark, distinguished sort of way, but seeing him like this made her kneecaps melt, along with most of the rest of her.

Did he have to pull the words from her mouth? he wondered in exasperation. "That I look like an idiot."

That was the very last thought that would have passed through her mind. Very slowly, never taking her eyes off him, she moved her head from side to side. "Not any idiot I know."

"But an idiot," he pressed.

She was about to make a very vocal denial of that completely unmerited description. He looked gorgeous, not idiotic, but how did she phrase that without sounding as if she was willing to jump into bed with him? He was far too straitlaced to be on the receiving end of that kind of sentiment.

Even if it did vibrate in every vein in her body.

But she was mercifully spared from making any kind of a reply because, just then, Emily came running in in her nightgown. The look on her very serious young face fairly shouted that Jackie had done something unforgivable to her. Again.

However, whatever complaint was hot on her tongue vanished as she came to a skidding halt just inside the study, where she had tracked down both adults in the house.

Her eyes were wide as she looked up at her father. Recognition mingled with confusion, making her entirely uncertain. "Daddy?"

"Yes, it's me." Jack bit off the curse that hovered on his tongue, not wanting to subject Emily to the less than flattering thoughts that were now thriving inside his head. He'd begun to pull off the hat and wig when the awestruck look on Emily's face froze his hand in midmotion.

She looked every bit the little girl who had inadvertently stumbled into Neverland, only to find a dashing pirate in place of the malevolent Captain Hook. "Daddy, you look beautiful," she cried.

Zooey grinned, relieved that the pressure was off her. "Out of the mouths of babes." Her comment earned her a slightly confused look from Jack. Their eyes met and held for a long, pregnant moment. Zooey could have sworn the temperature in the room went up a whole ten degrees. She turned her attention to Emily, not because she was the girl's nanny, but because right now it was easier to look at her than at Jack. "Your daddy's going to be Jack Sparrow."

Emily seemed to accept the explanation, but it only raised another question for him. "And who the hel—heck is Jack Sparrow?"

You, Zooey thought. "He's a magical pirate in *Pirates of the Caribbean*," she explained.

The reference was vaguely familiar, but raised still more questions. Nothing, it seemed, was straightforward when it came to the children's nanny. "The Disney ride?"

"The movie," she corrected. "Johnny Depp played him." Maybe that would do it for him, Zooey thought. But judging from Jack's expression, very little had been cleared up. The man probably didn't watch movies, she thought. Something else to address. Eventually.

Zooey turned toward Emily. Time to bring in the big guns, she thought. "Your daddy doesn't think this is a good costume for him. He doesn't want to wear it."

Emily reacted just as she'd hoped the little girl would. "Oh please, Daddy, please wear it. You're beautiful," she repeated.

Zooey bent down to her level. "Yes, he is, isn't he?" And then she straightened again, confident that the battle of the pirate costume had gone her way. "Go on up back to bed, Emily," she instructed. "I'll be there in a few minutes to tuck you in again."

Forgetting why she'd come down in the first place, still looking at her father, Emily nodded, then hurried out of the room.

Jack looked at Zooey as Emily disappeared down the hall. She couldn't begin to read his expression. "You don't play fair."

Zooey relaxed and grinned. She'd won the battle. "I never claimed I did. You do look very good, you know." And then a thought struck her and she sobered just a shade. "I'm sure Rebecca will think so."

"Rebecca?" he repeated, puzzled. "How is she going to see me?" He had no intention of leaving the premises in this outfit, even if the house caught on fire. He'd just resign himself to dying in the blaze.

"I invited her to the party." It hadn't been easy, but Rebecca did live only three doors down. Inviting everyone *else* on the block and omitting her would have made her seem petty and jealous.

Jack stared at her. "But she doesn't have any children."

Which was a technicality Zooey had almost given in to. But then, she was also inviting Bo and Carly to the party, and neither of them had children, either.

"No, but she is a neighbor and the party is for the adults in the neighborhood as well as the children." Zooey smiled up at him. "I thought that maybe Emily wasn't the only one who needed help with social skills."

She'd gone too far again. "You're their nanny, not mine."

His dark tone did not succeed in scaring her off. "Consider it a bonus."

Maybe being blunt was the only thing she'd understand, the only way to make her retreat. "I consider it irritating."

She paused for a moment, debating backing off. But that went against her grain. So, for the second time within the space of a few minutes, she stood up to him.

"You're within your rights to—"

Jack closed his eyes for a second, gathering strength and being grateful that he wasn't facing her in a courtroom. Because he'd be sorely tempted to wring her neck.

"Fire you—yes, I know." He opened his eyes again and gave her a meaningful look. "I just might take you up on that someday."

Her expression never changed. "I know."

"And still you continue." She was either very dumb or a hell of a poker player. He had a hunch it was the latter.

To her, it was a simple matter. "Have to be true to my nature."

"Of being a pest?" he demanded.

Zooey never blinked an eye. "Of doing what I think needs doing."

The woman was nothing short of infuriating, eating up his entire supply of patience.

Damn, but he wanted to kiss her.

To kiss her and shut that mouth of hers with his own so that he could just lose himself in her.

What the hell was the matter with him? This wasn't like him. The hat and wig were probably cutting off his circulation, he thought darkly.

That didn't change the fact that he wanted Zooey. That he wanted to make love with her.

He needed space. Needed to open a window and air out her scent, which was driving him crazy. It was raining outside, but the damp, dank breeze would be welcomed right about now.

"You promised to tuck Emily in."

"I know."

"I think you'd better go do that," he told her, his voice strained.

Go, leave. Before I do something stupid, Zooey, he pleaded silently.

Zooey smiled serenely at him, as if she'd heard his thoughts.

"On my way," she responded.

She left the room and Jack immediately crossed to the window, opening it and trying to erase her presence.

Chapter Eleven

Emily burst into Jack's study the following Saturday morning. "Daddy, Daddy, we're going shopping for stuff. You wanna come with us?" she asked him excitedly as his door banged open.

Jack winced inwardly, anticipating the hole in the wall that the doorknob probably made. He was going to have to start locking his door, he decided as he set down the brief he was reviewing. "Now why would I want to do that?"

"Because it's for the party. We're going to the *super*market!" she announced, emphasizing *super* because today that seemed to her like a particularly funny thing to call the grocery store.

Having raced into the room like gang-busters, Emily was now tugging on his arm with all her less than considerable might, trying to get him to stand up.

His daughter seemed a lot happier these days, Jack mused. A lot more lively. In true you-never-know-what-you're-missing-until-it's-gone fashion, he found himself missing the quieter Emily. But he knew that this change was actually for the best as far as the little girl was concerned.

Looking over her head, he saw Zooey standing in the doorway, a firm grip locked around Jackie's hand. For once, it appeared as if this invasion was not of her making.

"We have to go, Emily. Your daddy's busy," Zooey told her kindly.

"No, I'm not."

He could see that his response completely floored Zooey. In what was undoubtedly an unguarded moment, surprise registered on her face. Though he knew it was probably childish, he felt a small sense of accomplishment for being able to get to her. It seemed only fair, seeing as how the woman kept getting to him.

"You're not?" She was looking at the papers in his hand.

"Less than usual," he acknowledged.

Letting Jackie into the room ahead of her, Zooey crossed to Jack's desk. The same desk Jackie was attempting to scale. She caught the little boy up in her arms without missing a beat and set him down again, blocking his access.

She looked at Jack uncertainly, wondering what had brought this sudden change. "And you're willing to come to the supermarket with us?"

Emily was standing next to him, closer than a shadow. He passed his hand over her silky hair and she looked up at him, beaming. Emily, like her brother, had been unplanned. But he was beginning to understand why people wanted children.

"Might be interesting."

"Might be," Zooey echoed, still a little stunned. And then, because she couldn't help herself, she asked, "Are they putting something extra into your coffee these days?"

He was toying with her, he realized. And enjoying it. "Can't a man want to go with his family to the grocery store without being held suspect?"

With his family.

Had he just lumped her into the group by accident, or by design? Zooey felt her pulse accelerating.

Don't get ahead of yourself, Zooey. You don't want to go on a toboggan ride and find out there's no snow on the hill.

"Absolutely," she answered. Getting Jack to come along would have been her idea, except that she remembered what today was. And where he was going to be in a few hours. And with whom. "But I thought you might be wanting to get ready."

She couldn't mean for the party. That was tomorrow. Which left him fresh out of guesses. "For?"

Why was he making her say it? He couldn't possibly be that absentminded. Which only meant that he was having fun at her expense. And yet he didn't seem like the type. He wasn't cruel, just removed.

"Your date with Rebecca," Zooey finally said, once again taking Jackie away from a source of temptation—this time the coffee table. It had a glass top and she could almost see the thoughts going through the two-year-old's head. "It is today, isn't it?"

He'd canceled his date several days ago. It

didn't seem fair to him to take up Rebecca's time when his head was elsewhere and his heart just wasn't in it. But he'd had no intention of making a major announcement about his change of plans. "It was."

"Who's Rebecca?" Emily asked, looking from her father to Zooey.

"Was?" Zooey echoed. *Don't start celebrating, he's probably just rescheduling, that's all.* Still, even though she managed to keep the smile off her face, she couldn't quite manage to keep it out of her voice. "What happened?"

He was not about to go into detail, especially not around his children. "Can we talk about this later?" This time he was the one who took Jackie down from the sofa, where the child was attempting to build up momentum bouncing up and down on the cushions.

"Who's Rebecca?" Emily asked again, a little more forcefully.

"Just a lady in the neighborhood," Zooey told her. "She lives three doors down, close to Olivia. She'll be at the party."

Planting his son on the floor, Jack went to retrieve his coat. "I wouldn't count on it." He tossed the comment over his shoulder on the way.

Zooey caught Jackie's hand and drew the boy out of the room, following Jack. Emily came skipping along behind.

Now he'd done it, Zooey thought. The man had stirred up her curiosity until it was practically at the explosion level—and then just walked out. And he knew it. He'd been around her long enough to know that she was insatiably curious.

How could he do that to her?

But she knew that he wasn't about to discuss the matter around Emily and Jackie. She was just going to have to contain herself until she got him alone.

The next few hours, she thought, were going to be a mixture of ecstasy and agony.

He felt drained.

But oddly satisfied.

Pulling into his driveway, Jack realized that he was smiling to himself. He'd actually enjoyed the exhausting afternoon. Looking back, he couldn't remember the last time he'd been inside a supermarket. Foraging for groceries had never really numbered among his required tasks.

The last time he'd gone questing for food without intentionally winding up with a menu propped in front of him had been back in college. Before then, in his mother's house, there had been housekeepers to take care of that kind of thing. And afterward, there'd been Patricia. Grocery shopping was just something she took care of without involving him. After Patricia had died, the nannies he'd hired had taken care of stocking the refrigerator and the pantry.

This afternoon, with his squeaking grocery cart and his marauding children, had been nothing short of a near-life-altering experience.

He glanced at Zooey as he turned off the ignition. The music coming from the radio died down. His kids didn't. It seemed to him that they had been going nonstop since they left the house.

Unbuckling his seat belt, he got out of the car and went to open the trunk. He liked the sound of Zooey's laugh, he decided as he picked up four bags and carted them into the house. Jack made his way to the kitchen, where he deposited the bags on the table.

Behind him, Emily and Jackie were bringing up the rear, each proudly carrying a small plastic bag. Zooey had given Jackie the sack with the Halloween napkins. Emily had been awarded the colorful paper cups and plates to take in.

Looking at them now, he caught himself thinking that it felt very much like a family effort.

Or what a family effort would have felt like if he'd been familiar with such a thing, he amended. When Patricia was still alive, they'd never done anything as a family unit. She'd taken care of the kids, and on those rare occasions when he had some free time available, he and Patricia would get together to do something. It never extended beyond that, never included the children.

He'd been very close to being a stranger to his own children when Patricia died, he thought. The fault was his, he knew, but it didn't change the facts.

Today had been different.

What would it be like, he wondered as he went back to the car to retrieve the rest of the bags, if Zooey really was part of the family? If she was more than just the kids' nanny?

She *was* more than just the nanny, he reminded himself. Because they hadn't been a family until she'd come along. Just a man with two children he'd inherited from his late wife. It was Zooey who'd orchestrated things to get him closer to the kids. Pulling him into it, something that Patricia had never managed to accomplish. If that had ever been her goal.

Looking back now, he wasn't sure. He'd married Patricia with the greatest of hopes that he'd found someone who could finally make him feel. But ultimately, that wasn't enough, and somehow, somewhere down the line, those feelings he'd thought he had just seemed to vanish. Fading slowly until he gradually became aware of the fact that they weren't there at all.

That maybe he had just imagined them.

But now—now they seemed to be back. Stronger than they had ever been before.

And, ironically, he needed to bank them down. Because whatever it was he was feeling couldn't be allowed to go any further. Couldn't be allowed to thrive and grow. For so many reasons.

He'd never liked complications, and at the very least, getting involved with Zooey promised a whole host of complications.

Walking in with the last four grocery bags, he deposited them on the table. Miraculously, Zooey had unpacked all the others and put the contents away, except for one. He watched her now as she placed four cans of pumpkin pie mix on the counter, right beside the stack of unbaked pie crusts.

"You're really going to bake all those pies?" he asked skeptically.

"Sure. And I'm going to have help, aren't I?" Her question was addressed to Emily and Jackie, who both nodded vigorously.

"Yes!" Emily cried.

"Yes!" Jackie echoed with deafening enthusiasm.

"Well, that should set you back a few hours," Jack commented with a laugh. In his opinion, Zooey was undertaking a monumental task. "'You're a better man than I am, Gunga Din.'"

She began to take bowls out of the cupboards below the counter. "Rudyard Kipling notwithstanding, it will go very smoothly." Measuring cups came out of another cupboard. Mixing spoons emerged from a drawer in the corner. "The key to getting things done when you have children around is utilizing them, not trying to get them to stay out of your way."

"If you say so."

Zooey grinned. "You're welcome to pitch in if you like."

He looked at the items she was setting out.

The closest he ever came to cooking was eating. He knew nothing about what it took to transform raw goods into edible offerings. "I thought I already had, by agreeing to wear that ridiculous costume."

If an inch was offered, she felt confident that somewhere there was a mile waiting to be taken. Or at least coaxed into the open. "That was a start."

Wasn't she ever satisfied? "You don't want much, do you, woman?"

"No more than I think I can get." An enigmatic smile played on her lips. She turned toward Emily and Jackie. "Kids, why don't you go change your clothes and wash your hands so you can help me bake the pies? Emily, help your brother," she added.

With a patient sigh, Emily took his hand. "Come on, Jackie."

To Jack's surprise, the little boy docilely followed her out. Miracles apparently came in all sizes these days.

He glanced at the preparations Zooey was making. "Party's tomorrow," he pointed out. "Why bake the pies today?"

Opening the pantry, she took an apron from its hook and slipped the loop over her head, then began tying the strings behind her back. "Because I don't like leaving things—"

"To the last minute." He laughed, shaking his head. "Yes, I'm beginning to get the idea."

The second Jackie disappeared down the hall behind his sister, Zooey turned to look at Jack. She had been patient long enough, and not knowing was killing her. "Why aren't you going out tonight?"

Jack looked at her, stunned. They'd been shopping for close to two hours. He'd forgotten all about the conversation he'd left hanging earlier in the study. Obviously, she hadn't.

"You're like a junkyard dog, aren't you? Once you clamp down, you don't stop."

Zooey shrugged. She'd been called worse. "I would have preferred a more flattering comparison, but, okay, I won't argue with the image," she stated, then focused on him. "Why?"

He wasn't comfortable discussing his social life with her. Especially since she was both the reason why he'd first gone out with Rebecca and the reason he'd canceled his date tonight. "Don't you think that's a little too personal for you to ask?"

"Probably," she agreed. But that didn't stop her from wanting to know. "Why?" she repeated for the third time, pinning him with her eyes.

He knew by now that she wasn't going to let up until he gave her some kind of reason. "Because I don't believe in wasting a person's time."

Zooey's eyes narrowed. "Yours or hers?"

He paused for a second before answering. Wondering if he should. "Both."

Zooey studied the man standing beside her at the counter for a long moment. She read what she needed to into his answer. And then she smiled. Broadly.

"I see."

"No, you don't," Jack informed her firmly. He didn't want her to get the wrong—or in this case, right—idea. This was a matter between him and him, and no one else.

The more he denied it, the more certain Zooey was that she was right.

"Yeah," she countered, feeling immensely pleased. "I do." As she waited for Emily and Jackie to return, she folded the last of the grocery bags and put them away for future use, then crossed to the sink to wash her hands. "How are you at grating cheese?" she asked nonchalantly. *He's not going out with Rebecca. He's staying in. Home team 1, Vixens 0.*

"Cheese?" he echoed uncertainly. "For the pie?"

He really didn't know anything about cooking or baking, did he? She refrained from pointing out that there was no cheese in pumpkin pie. She didn't want to alienate him or insult him, especially not since he was back on the market.

"No," she replied sweetly, "for the stuffed tenderloin I'm making."

No more enlightened now than he had been a minute ago, Jack lifted his shoulders and then let them drop again in a mute indication of helplessness. "I don't know, I've never tried."

She would have guessed as much. "Now's as good a time as any to learn." Taking the cheese grater out of the utility drawer, she presented it, a cutting board and a hunk of mozzarella cheese to Jack. "Have at it," she urged. She put the grater into his right hand, the cheese into his left and slipped the board closer to him on the counter. "Just be sure to watch your fingers," she cautioned. "Blood isn't part of the recipe." As Jackie and Emily ran in, making their return appearance, she switched her attention to them. "Okay, everyone's here," she announced cheerfully. "Let's get to work."

Jack thought of the brief he had waiting in the study. It wasn't urgent, just something he'd planned on getting done before Sunday night and the much-dreaded Halloween party.

But it would keep, he thought as thin slivers of cheese began to make their appearance at the bottom of the grater, forming a small, growing mound. It would definitely keep.

The doorbell started ringing a little after five the next evening as party guests began to make their appearance.

Coming down the stairs, feeling awkward as hell, Jack hardly recognized his own house. Zooey and the kids had spent all morning and part of the afternoon decorating. Now there was hardly any space that didn't have a friendly ghost, a warm fuzzy spider or some mythical, equally happy-looking creature hovering against a backdrop of balloons.

There was candy everywhere, and somehow, miraculously, Zooey managed to keep Jackie out of it. To that end, she'd enlisted Emily's help. Honor bound, Emily had to refrain from eating the candy herself.

His daughter apparently had more willpower than he gave her credit for.

As for Zooey, the woman was nothing short of a witch, despite the harem girl costume she'd slipped on at the last minute. Even though she had all but forced him to parade around in his costume, she hadn't shown him hers. So when he caught a glimpse of her coming out of the kitchen carrying the punch bowl, Jack had found himself in dire jeopardy of swallowing his tongue. Or of carrying on a flirtation with cardiac arrest.

He'd never seen material arranged so sensuously. Everything essential was covered, but alluringly so. The costume fired up his imagination to the point that he found himself indulging in fantasies. Fantasies he knew he couldn't bring to fruition, but that nonetheless gave him no respite.

"Wow."

When he heard the single word, he realized that he hadn't just thought it, he'd uttered it. The flash of an appreciative grin as she turned to look at him told Jack that Zooey had heard his verbal error.

"Thank you. Right back at you. You look very dashing," she countered.

He scowled. His scalp was itchy beneath

the wig, and the hat was making him perspire. "I look ridiculous," he declared.

It wasn't vanity prompting him, Zooey thought. He actually believed what he was saying. And obviously hadn't taken a look at the cartoon figures and comic book heroes milling around in his living room, which was growing progressively more festive.

"No, you don't," she insisted. Spying Emily, she called her over. When the little girl came running up, Zooey placed her hands on the child's shoulders and turned her around to face her father. "Doesn't your daddy look handsome, Emily?"

Emily nodded vigorously, the ringlets that Zooey had spent half an hour setting into her hair bobbing like golden springs. But before she could say anything, the doorbell rang.

Emily's eyes widened. Shifting from foot to foot, anxious to be gone, she asked hopefully, "Can I get it?"

As a rule, Zooey never allowed either of the children to open the door, evoking the do-not-trust-strangers mandate.

"We're all home," Zooey told her, emphasizing her point. "So it's okay."

But even though they lived in a neighborhood that was deemed to be one of the safest in the state, that did not automatically give Emily a green light to open the door whenever someone came knocking or ringing. Zooey firmly believed it was better to teach good behavior than to have to negate and "unteach" bad habits.

Dressed as a fairy princess, Emily ran over to the door, the veil from her small, pointed hat flapping behind her like a pink cape.

"Nice job," Jack observed.

Zooey thought he was referring to the costume she'd made. She'd finished it just this morning. Actually, she had sewn all three of their costumes, including Jackie's Robin Hood outfit. Only Jack's was left up to professionals. She'd tried to control as much as she could, making sure that Jack had no viable excuse why he couldn't dress up for his children's party.

"Thanks," she responded, watching the door to see who Emily was admitting. She watched Olivia bounce into the room, wearing a poodle skirt and saddle shoes, with her hair pulled back into a swinging ponytail. Cute. "It was remarkably simple to make," she said, referring to Emily's costume.

"No, I meant telling her about when she could open the door and when she couldn't."

There was an admiration in his eyes as he looked at her. "You've been very good for the kids."

No hardship there, she thought. Part of the trick was just remembering how she'd wanted to be treated when she was Emily's age. With respect, not ordered around as if she didn't have her own set of brains.

"They've been very good for *me*," she told him. "Actually, they have a rather calming influence," she confided.

Jack could only stare at her, unable to comprehend how that was possible. And then he laughed, really laughed. He judged that, combined, his children probably had more energy than was typically generated on an average day at the nuclear power plant. That was *not* conducive to having a calming influence.

Zooey was one very strange, intriguing young woman. Not to mention sensual.

He banked down the last thought and went to greet his guests. Hoping no one would laugh.

Chapter Twelve

When he finally got to the front door and opened it, Jack wasn't prepared for what he saw standing there.

Instead of the trick-or-treaters who had been ringing his bell throughout the evening, it was yet another guest. He'd thought that everyone who was coming to the party had already arrived.

He hadn't counted on Rebecca attending after he'd canceled their date without rescheduling.

And he definitely hadn't counted on her looking like this.

There was an amused expression on her

face, undoubtedly in reaction to the surprised, unsettled one on his. But he could hardly be faulted for that.

At first glance, Rebecca appeared to be wearing a very long, flowing blond wing. And nothing else.

The hair extended down to her knees and was, mercifully, strategically arranged to cover everything that was supposed to be covered. Just barely. The operative word here, he thought, being *barely*.

His first impulse was to grab one of the coats from the coatrack and throw it over her.

"Aren't you going to invite me in?" Rebecca's amusement grew by the moment.

"Um, yes. Sure." Jack moved back awkwardly, as if all his joints had suddenly been fused together.

Entering, Rebecca moved aside so that he could close the door again. She was very aware of the looks she was garnering. And reveling in it.

"I thought lawyers were never at a loss for words." And then, since she'd gotten the hoped-for reaction from him, her smile became benevolent. "Relax, Jack. I've got a body stocking on. A very thick body stocking," she emphasized mischievously. "In case you haven't figured it out yet, I'm supposed to be Lady Godiva." The look in her eyes became positively wicked. "I just seem to have misplaced my horse."

From out of nowhere, and to his eternal gratitude, Zooey materialized with a tray of hors d'oeuvres. She placed the tray between him and Rebecca, her smile never fading as she greeted the party's newest guest.

"I'm sure your 'horse' will turn up somewhere, Rebecca. Maybe he's just taking a breather for a moment," she suggested, never taking her eyes off the other woman. She thrust the tray closer to her. "Crab puff?"

Rebecca glanced down at the tray, but then shook her head. Her hair moved ever so slightly. "Maybe later."

"They're going quickly," Zooey told her, addressing her words to Rebecca's back as the woman melted into the gathering. "There might not be any left later." Turning to look at Jack, Zooey asked mildly, "Would you like a tank of oxygen?"

Having collected himself, and relieved that the woman wasn't actually wearing an X-rated outfit— because there were children to consider, especially his own—Jack shrugged away her question as casually as he could. "I just didn't think that she was coming."

Obviously, Zooey thought. She was surprised when he didn't crane his neck, following Rebecca's progress. Maybe there really *wasn't* anything going on between them. Zooey found that extremely heartening.

She laughed softly at his naive assumption about Rebecca's attendance. "And miss a chance to mingle with the men in the neighborhood? Don't know much about women, do you?"

"No," he admitted, popping a crab puff into his mouth. It was gone in one bite. "I don't."

His admission took her by surprise. One of the guests reached over to snare a crab puff and Zooey raised the tray a little to make the transfer easier. "An honest lawyer. Wow, you are unique."

"And hungry," Jack told her, taking two more crab puffs. He nodded appreciatively. "These are good."

The compliment pleased her, though she tried not to show it. She'd baked them from scratch. "If you want something more substantial, there's the tenderloin," she reminded him. "It's on the table in the dining room. I could get you some."

"That's okay." He indicated the last crab puff in his hand. "This'll hold me for a while."

"Okay, then, time to push the crab puffs some more," she quipped.

Jack watched as she made her way through the colorful, milling groups of guests in the family room and beyond. Without missing a beat, Zooey had easily taken on the duties of a hostess for this party. He would have said it was her waitressing training rising to the fore, except that, by her own admission, she'd been a fairly poor waitress.

No, it was something more. Something inherent. Because there she was, effortlessly weaving in and out of the crowd with a tray of food in her hands, stopping to exchange a few words with this neighbor or that, as if she'd been throwing and hostessing parties all of her life.

He heard her laugh at something that Megan Schumacher, Olivia's aunt, said to her. The sound managed to travel to him above the din of mingled adult voices and squealing children. It seemed to go right through him, burrowing into all the corners of his being.

With effort, he turned his attention elsewhere. Anywhere but where Zooey was.

Carly and Bo were over in a corner. The newlyweds had their heads together, talking, touching, laughing like two teenagers in love. They seemed oblivious to everyone else around them.

Jack popped the last crab puff into his mouth, hardly aware of what he was doing. Aware only that he envied Bo, envied the man what he had to be feeling right now. He had no doubts, judging by Bo's expression, that his gut was probably tightening and he was finding breathing to be a challenge because his heart was pounding so hard.

Startled, Jack stopped. *He* had experienced those very same symptoms recently. Not at the door just now when Rebecca made her appearance. Not even when he'd taken the woman out those two times, or on their second date, which had ended with an unambiguous invitation to come inside her house and remain for breakfast. It had nothing at all to do with Rebecca.

He'd felt all those things, and more, when he had kissed Zooey.

He needed, he decided, a drink.

And something to take his mind off Zooey and the way her hips moved as she continued to make her way through the crowd.

Jack went in search of someone to talk to. Preferably someone with a major supply of testosterone.

* * *

"This was a wonderful idea, Zooey," Angela Schumacher enthused as she took the next to last crab puff on the tray Zooey offered. She looked toward her three kids, or rather, looked around for them. Each was with his or her own peers, and for once, no one was arguing. Moments like this were close to perfect for her. "The kids are having a great time."

Zooey had never doubted it for a moment. All she'd really needed to do was provide the refreshments and the games. The kids took it from there. And most were generally well behaved. She was keeping an eye on the ones who tended to disrupt things.

"And the adults?" Zooey prompted, glancing from Angela to her sister. Megan had temporarily left her fiancé, Greg Banning, second in command at Banning Enterprises, talking over the merits of forsaking daylight savings time with one of the other men while she got some punch.

Taking a cup, Megan ladled the fruity drink into it. "We're holding our own," she told Zooey. Reaching for a second cup, she nodded toward another couple. Adam Shibbs only had eyes for the very pregnant Molly

Jackson, whose side he seldom left. "Molly certainly looks happier these days than she has in a very long time."

"People in love generally tend to look that way," Angela commented a bit tersely.

Her tone was not lost on Zooey. "That sounded a little cynical."

Angela flushed, shifting uncomfortably. She hadn't meant to call attention to herself. But having been abandoned by her husband brought out something less than charitable within her.

"Did it?" she asked innocently. She decided to have a glass of punch herself, and waited for her sister to be finished. "Sorry," she murmured. "Old wounds just rising to the surface."

Zooey looked at her knowlingly. It was no secret what had happened to the woman. Her husband had walked out. Once out of the picture, the man became lax with his child support payments, forcing Angela to work extra hours in an effort to make up the difference. Which meant that her time with the children at what amounted to a vulnerable period in their lives had to be cut down. Fortunately, Megan was there to take up the slack, but when you got right down to it, it just wasn't the same thing.

Angela's kids wanted Angela. And she knew it.

"They only become old wounds if you let them heal," Zooey murmured. "Otherwise, they remain ongoing, open wounds."

"So now you're dispensing medical advice along with hors d'oeuvres?" Jack's voice came from directly behind her.

She swung around, surprised by his unexpected appearance and trying her best not to show it. It didn't jibe with the cool, calm and collected image she was attempting to portray tonight.

"Whatever it takes," Zooey replied nonchalantly. She set the now empty tray on the nearest flat surface and faced Jack. "Do you need me for something?"

He almost laughed out loud. If ever he'd been asked a loaded question, this was it. A dozen different answers, all variations of the same feeling, the same desire, materialized in his head in response to her innocent query.

Or maybe not so innocent, Jack amended, looking into Zooey's eyes. She seemed to know exactly what she was asking, he realized. Exactly what kind of response her question aroused.

He doubted it was possible for her to be ignorant of what she was doing to him just by breathing.

But because he hoped no one else was privy to this, he said, "I thought maybe you'd want to get the kids started playing their games. It looks to me like everyone's here."

Not trusting his assessment, Zooey conducted her own quick survey, and discovered he was actually right. There was surprise and admiration in her eyes. "You do keep track."

He saw Angela and Megan struggling not to laugh as they moved off to another area of the room.

"I'm a lawyer, Zooey," he said to her. "Credit me with a little bit of awareness."

"Oh, but I do," she told him, the soul of innocence. "Very little." And then she laughed at her own joke. The dark look on Jack's face brought her up short. Now what?

She didn't have long to wait. "Don't do that," he told her.

He'd lost her. She hadn't done anything. Not for the last five minutes. "Do what?"

"Laugh."

Okay, now he was getting just plain weird,

she thought. Just because he had trouble curving his mouth into a smile didn't mean she had to become solemn as well. This was a party. He *needed* to loosen up.

"Why?" she retorted, propping one hand on her waist.

His answer totally floored her, leaving her without a comeback.

"Because it gets to me," he told her tersely, just before he turned on his heel and walked toward a gathering comprised of a cowboy, an alien, a futuristic space traveler and Fred Flintstone. The group, all neighbors that he recognized and spoke to on occasion, looked very eclectic. It suited his mood.

Stopping only long enough to collect the last of the hors d'oeuvres from the kitchen and replenish her supply, Zooey made her way over to Molly Jackson and her fiancé, Adam Shibbs. The duo were dressed as Romeo and his ever-so-slightly pregnant Juliet.

Molly reached over to the tray without looking. Her attention was riveted to the boyish-looking, blond-haired Adam. Zooey had known the woman since starting her job with Jack, and had never seen Molly looking happier.

Why shouldn't she be? Zooey thought, retreating again. Molly was getting a baby *and* a husband, almost at the same time. What could be better than that?

She watched as Rebecca approached the couple, moving to hug Molly and say something to Adam. Both greeted her warmly. Zooey recalled that Rebecca had thrown Molly a baby shower just last month.

That meant the woman wasn't all bad, Zooey supposed. Actually, Rebecca wasn't really bad at all. Just in her space.

Her space.

Listen to her, Zooey mocked herself. As if Jack Lever was hers. As if the man would actually have anything to do with an ex-waitress, an ex-dog walker, currently a nanny who, if the truth be told, was having trouble finding where her head really belonged.

Her heart, however, was another matter. Zooey knew where her heart belonged, or at least was.

Even if it shouldn't be.

Rousing herself, she abandoned thoughts that were going to lead her nowhere, and got back to overseeing the party and making sure everyone was having fun. Even Rebecca.

Zooey had no concerns as to whether Megan, Angela's sister, was enjoying herself. It was obvious she was, even to the casual observer.

Megan had arrived dressed as a fairy godmother, right down to the wand.

"Actually," the graphic artist had confided a few minutes earlier, "I feel more like Cinderella. Especially every time I look at Greg." A contented sigh, tinged with a hint of disbelief, accompanied the admission. "I'm surprised I'm not black-and-blue from pinching myself."

"That's supposed to be a figurative statement," Zooey had told her with an amused laugh.

Megan appeared lost in her own thoughts as she continued gazing toward Greg. Even dressed as one of the Musketeers, he looked very Ivy League.

"Who would have ever thought that a plain Jane like me would have landed someone like that?"

The one thing Zooey couldn't abide was listening to people run themselves down. Especially someone she liked.

"Me. I would have thought," Zooey told her. "And just take a look at yourself." For lack of a mirror, she directed Megan toward her reflection in the sliding glass door that led out to the patio. "You're not a plain Jane anymore. And even when you thought you were, you weren't," she insisted. "There was always an inner glow about you, Megan," she pointed out. A shy, appreciative smile bloomed on Megan's face. "You just relaxed long enough to let it surface and come out."

Megan knew better than to offer any denials to what Zooey was saying; she just wouldn't accept them. But something else struck her. "You're a great one for dispensing advice."

"Yes," Zooey agreed, sensing something more was coming. "I am."

"What about you and Pulse-Accelerating Man?" Megan nodded toward where Jack was standing with a group of men.

"Jack?" Puzzled, she wasn't sure where Megan was going with this. "What about him?"

"He has his eye on you, you know," Megan told her.

"No, he doesn't," she said quickly. Because to entertain the hope that Megan might be right, and find out otherwise, would have been too cruelly disappointing. Better not to hope at all than to be crushed. "And even if he does, it's just to make sure that I'm doing what he pays me for."

Humor curved Megan's mouth. "You're taking money for that?"

"No!" Zooey retorted with feeling, then lowered her voice when she saw that she'd attracted attention she definitely didn't want. "I mean—he pays me for watching his children."

"Mothers watch children, too, you know."

The word *mother* stirred up an entire myriad of feelings inside of her, setting off thoughts she didn't feel equipped to deal with at the moment. Because in the dead of night, when restlessness plagued her, she'd found herself entertaining the idea of being Emily and Jackie's mother.

And Jack's wife…

Still, she was confident that no one would ever guess she thought about that. Zooey raised her head. "What are you saying?"

The smile on Megan's lips was kind. Understanding. "What do you think I'm saying?"

She didn't trust herself to answer, so she diverted the conversation by pointing out the obvious. "Jack was going out with Rebecca."

There were next to no secrets in the neighborhood. Everyone took a great deal of interest in everyone else. "But he's not anymore, is he?"

"No."

Megan put her hand over Zooey's and squeezed it warmly. "That's because someone closer to home has his attention."

No, she wasn't going to go there. She wasn't going to begin building castles in the air, much as she wanted to. "The only thing that has his attention on an ongoing basis are his briefs."

Laughter entered Megan's eyes. She'd changed a great deal in the last month or so, come out of her shell and grabbed life with both hands.

"Tell me about them."

"Not *those* kinds of briefs," Zooey hissed.

Megan stood back as if to get a better view of her. "I never thought it was possible."

"What?" Zooey demanded.

"You're blushing."

She could feel the heat rising along her neck, her cheeks. She had no doubt that Megan was right, but she wasn't about to admit it. "There are a lot of people here. The room's getting warmer."

Megan glanced to where Jack was standing. He was in the center of a group of men, yet completely separated from the conversation going on around him. And he was looking over toward them.

Toward Zooey.

"And with any luck," Megan commented, "it'll get warmer still after everyone leaves."

Zooey looked at her sharply. For one of the very few times in her life, she was flustered. "You don't know what you're talking about."

Her friend inclined her head, lowering her voice. "Trust me, Zooey, the people involved are sometimes the last to know." She glanced toward Greg. He was coming over to join her. Her eyes shone with love. "Believe me, I should know."

Zooey shook her head. Megan meant well, but her instincts were off.

She was happy for Megan. Very happy for all the couples here who had found love and were making the most of it. But you didn't find what you weren't looking for, and she wasn't looking for love. First she needed to get her life in order and on the right track, *then* she could find a place for love. Not before.

She realized that she was looking toward Jack and clutching the tray extra hard. With effort, she forced herself to blow out a breath and then take another one in. Slowly.

It was an evening that seemed to go on forever. Not that Zooey found it a hardship to endure. The party was nothing short of wonderful. She enjoyed people, and the folks who lived along Danbury Way were a very special lot, with the possible exception of the always-bickering Martins.

But they hadn't shown up, which was just as well. They weren't really missed, and everyone else, with or without children, had responded positively to the Halloween party invitation. So much so that the original planned sit-down dinner had to be turned into a stand-up buffet. The kids loved it, gathering together whenever they wanted and eating when the mood hit.

That eventually translated into an incredible amount of paper plates, cups, napkins and miscellaneous garbage strewn around the entire first floor of the house, and the grounds outside by those hardy enough to brave the sudden drop in temperature. It was all worth it.

The exodus began at eight and continued until almost eleven. The discrepancy in time depended on whether or not guests had children to take home.

Cleanup was an ongoing process that didn't seem to get done, despite the help Zooey received from Angela, Megan, Carly, Molly and, surprisingly, from Rebecca. Before they left, the women did, however, put a sizable dent in what she was going to have to face tomorrow.

She was still finding stray glasses and plates to pick up even as the last of the guests walked out.

"Leave it," Jack told her after he closed the door.

Emily and Jackie had long since been put to bed, and the house suddenly seemed almost eerily quiet.

Zooey continued gathering. "I just thought I'd do a little more now—"

Crossing over to her, Jack physically took the paper plates out of her hands.

"I said leave it, Zooey," he repeated. "You've done more than enough." He glanced around. The house looked almost clean to him. "Call in one of those cleaning crews tomorrow to handle the rest."

She hated wasting money. "There's no need, Jack, I can—"

He frowned, stopping dead in his tracks. "Do you feel an overwhelming need to contradict everything I say?"

"No. Not an overwhelming need," she replied, a smile creeping over her lips. "Just when you're wrong—"

He cut her short. "Humor me. Call in a cleaning crew. Your time is far too valuable to waste picking up paper plates."

She liked that he thought so, but wasn't sure if that was the punch or the man talking. She needed to be clear. "I thought that was what you were paying me for. Being the nanny-slash-housekeeper."

He laughed shortly. "I don't want to wear you out before your time."

There was little chance of that. If the kids hadn't done it by now, a little elbow grease wasn't about to do the job.

"I'm more resilient than I look."

He gazed at her for a long moment. When he spoke, his voice was low. "I already know that."

Damn, there went her heart again. In double time. "Oh?"

"Yes, 'oh,'" he echoed.

How she came to be in his arms the next minute, Jack couldn't have explained. He had no memory of making the first move, no memory of folding his arms around her. All he knew was that time seemed to suddenly stop of its own accord.

Because her presence was filling the room.

Chapter Thirteen

Even as he kissed her, Jack knew it was
wrong. Knew that he should have more control over himself, more willpower than this.

But the sad truth of it was, he didn't. When
it came to the feelings that Zooey stirred up,
his willpower, his resolve, his whatever it was
that ordinarily kept him on the straight and
narrow, unwavering path, were badly cor-
roded. Moreover, the very foundations of that
willpower had been turned, by this mere slip
of a woman, from concrete to Swiss cheese,
so that simply taking her into his arms, simply kissing her, was setting off an entire chain
reaction inside him that he couldn't control.

He could only stand here in mystified confusion and feel it unfold.

The effects were heightened when Zooey rose up on her toes, wrapped her arms around his neck, leaned into him and deepened the kiss. It was as if she'd been waiting for this to happen all evening long.

If so, that made two of them.

But still, it shouldn't *be* happening. He wasn't some reckless teenager, governed by mindless impulse, by raging hormones. Hell, he'd never *had* raging hormones. He hadn't behaved this way when he actually was a teenager, so why was he doing so now, surrendering to his emotions as an adult? He was a lawyer, for God's sake, a man who his colleagues said was the last word in steely control.

Where was that steely control now, when he really needed it?

With what felt like his last ounce of swiftly dwindling strength, Jack managed to take hold of Zooey's shoulders and pull back.

His brain vainly searched for a way to frame an apology. Because he owed her one for misleading her this way. For making her think that this was about something other than just gratifying a physical urge. Because it couldn't be about anything else.

He searched her face, looking for a sign, for a way to ease into this. But all he saw was exactly the opposite. "Zooey, I didn't mean—"

The look in Zooey's green eyes told him she had his number, but good.

"Yes," she whispered, "you did. And so did I."

She was right. But going forward, as everything inside of him begged him to, could very possibly destroy that newly constructed haven that not only he, but more importantly, his children, had taken up residence in. He needed to make Zooey understand that. To understand that while she was precious to him, to all of them, nothing could be allowed to happen here.

He threaded his fingers through her hair. Desire pounded its fists against him. He was having trouble trying to ignore everything but the right course to take. "Zooey, you've come to mean a great deal to Jackie and to Emily, of course—"

And they, Zooey thought, had come to mean a great deal to her. Almost from the first moment in the coffee shop that morning he'd brought them in. More than she could even put into words.

But this wasn't about Emily or Jackie, this was about Jack. About them.

Or was she just deluding herself?

She'd never been one to hang back, to wonder if there was rain or sunshine outside her door. She wasn't the type to find out by listening to a weather report, or staying safely indoors while looking through a window. Zooey was proud of the fact that she'd always thrown open the door and braved whatever it was that was waiting outside for her.

This was no different.

"And you?" she pressed, her eyes never leaving his. "Do I mean a great deal to you?"

How did he answer that and stay true to the goal he'd set for himself? And how could he accomplish that without hurting Zooey? He felt like a man in an uncharted minefield.

"Having you here… Having you here…"

He was trying to say that having her here, taking care of his children the way she did, afforded him peace of mind. It allowed him to function and do what he did best. But right now, having her here *didn't* allow him to function. It didn't even allow him to think, or talk like a man with half a brain. Having her here at this moment was scrambling his thoughts, his pulse, setting absolutely everything on its ear.

His voice had trailed off and he didn't look as if he was going to finish what he'd begun to say. "Yes?" Zooey murmured.

Frustration all but exploded in his veins. "Oh, the hell with it," he growled. The next second he lowered his mouth back to hers.

Oh, the hell with it. The words echoed in her head. Not exactly an endearment, Zooey thought, surrendering to the feeling Jack summoned from within her. And definitely not the tender words a woman waited to hear. But in an odd way, she understood the sentiment behind the frustration that had caused him to say it.

Understood it because it was rampaging through her own body.

She wanted to make love with him. Desperately. To have him touch her and take what was already his.

But even as everything suddenly went on overload inside of her, Zooey knew that they couldn't give in to the demands raging within them. Or at least, not where they currently were, standing beside the buffet table. They were right out in the open down here, and

Emily and Jackie had a habit of popping up where least expected. Zooey didn't want to take a chance on setting their sex education back by a couple of decades.

But God, she wanted him. Wanted Jack so much that in another moment there wasn't going to be a shred of logic left in her head.

"Wait." It took everything within her to voice the cry, to make him stop just as he cupped her breast and sent all sorts of delicious sensations coursing madly through her system.

At the sound of her voice, everything pulled up short inside of him. He knew it. Damn it, he knew. Knew he should have somehow harnessed himself. Knew he'd gone too far.

He jerked back as if someone had jabbed a red-hot poker in his chest. "Zooey, I'm sorry. I shouldn't have—"

Why did he think she was saying no? Did he think she was some kind of mercurial tease? Someone who ran hot and cold almost simultaneously? She just wanted a change of venue, not of agenda.

"My room," she instructed breathlessly.

Jack stared at her. His brain wasn't processing. "Your room?"

Maybe he had something against doing it

there. It didn't matter where they did it as long as the children couldn't see them.

"Or yours. I don't care, but please, take me somewhere." *Before I implode or explode, or go all to pieces.* "Just not here," she added. She ran the tip of her tongue along her bottom lip, tasting him. "The children might…"

Damn it, how could he have been so stupid? So self-absorbed and overwhelmed that he had forgotten Emily and Jackie could wake up and come wandering out of their rooms and down the stairs at any second?

He might be a hell of a lawyer, but he was one sad example of what a father should be.

"I—"

Zooey put her finger to his lips, silencing anything he might have to say. She didn't want to hear any further attempts at an apology, didn't want anything to take away from the magic of the moment. Grasping his hand, she led Jack to the staircase.

At the foot of the stairs, just as she was about to lead the way up, Zooey suddenly found her feet leaving the floor. Jack had lifted her into his arms. She looked at him in surprise.

He resisted the temptation to kiss her again.

The fact that her weight barely registered was a source of concern to him.

"Don't you eat?" he demanded. He hardly ever saw her take more than two bites in succession before she was up on her feet, attending to something. "You don't weigh anything."

Zooey winked at him. "I do it all with smoke and mirrors." She slipped her arms around his neck, thinking how nice this felt. Still, something within her prompted her to make a token protest. "I can walk."

"I know. I've seen you." He also knew that given half a chance, Zooey would take complete charge of the situation, and a man needed to take the lead sometime.

This was that sometime.

Because this was going to happen. There was no point in pretending it wouldn't. It was almost as if it was meant to, and the longer it was put off, the larger the resulting explosion threatened to be.

If his logic proved to be faulty, he'd examine it tomorrow, in the light of day, when all secrets were exposed. All he knew was that in the soft glow of evening, he couldn't resist her any longer.

There was something about Zooey, some

undefinable X factor that spoke to him, that jumped up and seized him by the throat, threatening to cut off his air supply permanently if he didn't immerse himself in her.

A man couldn't live very long without his air supply.

Jack brought Zooey into his bedroom, closing the door with his elbow. The click echoed in the quiet room as he set her down at the foot of his king-size bed.

The moment he did, they came together, sealed to one another. Their bodies sent waves of heat shooting in all directions as his mouth once again closed over hers.

His hands roamed her body as if to reassure him that she was actually there, that he was actually touching her.

There was a breathlessness to it, to just being with her like this. Drowning in her.

Anticipating more.

There were no buttons on his shirt, Zooey realized. That made it easier. The material was loose and billowing and she managed to get it up over his head and off his body with a minimum of effort. His vest was already mysteriously gone, shed somewhere between the family room and the front door.

The moment she dropped his shirt from her

fingers, Zooey was certain she understood what a piece of toast unable to pop out of the toaster felt like. Just looking at him caused heat to radiate, nonstop, all over her. Doubling her body temperature and threatening to turn her into a piece of charcoal.

Her breathing was quick, shallow, and growing more so as she felt his hands on her. He was removing her veils, trying to get down to her bare skin.

"How many layers does this thing have?" There was exasperation in Jack's voice.

"Just one less than enough to make you insane," she told him.

One by one, the veils came off, leaving her vulnerable and wanting. The colorful scarves floated to the floor, creating a rainbow of fabric around them.

Zooey shivered as she felt his strong, capable hands on her bare hips. She caught her breath as he tugged down the harem pants, leaving her in thong underwear that was all but transparent.

And then in nothing at all, wearing only his hot gaze.

He had the same feeling he'd had when he'd first looked at a sculpture of Venus while on a forced field trip to the Metropolitan Museum of Art years ago. Overwhelmed. Awed.

Zooey's body, devoid of clothing, was tight and sleek and firm. And he wanted her so badly he could barely breathe.

This time when he kissed her, each kiss was more powerful than before, collecting momentum from the last, flowering into the next. Unable to keep still, his hands continued to roam almost worshipfully over her, touching, sampling, wanting.

And all the while, Jack kissed her over and over again, completely absorbed by what he was doing. Immersed in the sight, the sound, the scent of her. Nothing else existed beyond that. Nothing else registered, save how soft her skin felt, how pliant her body was, and how, as she twisted and turned beneath him on his large, lonely bed, she sent tongues of fire shooting into his every single pore.

Fueling him.

Inspiring him.

Unaccountably, Jack found himself doing things he'd never thought of doing, not even with Patricia.

Patricia had been a good woman. A good wife. But their lovemaking had been unimaginative, right from the very beginning. He blamed himself for that. Pursuit of his career had taken all his energy. To appease the woman he'd married, he'd gone through all the required motions, the tried-and-true steps. They'd brought him to the desired conclusion, but left him unsatisfied. As they'd probably left her.

But with Zooey, it was different. With Zooey, there were firecrackers. There were sparklers going off, lighting up the dark skies with wonder and an endless fountain of elation.

He was certain he was dreaming. Imagining all of it.

And yet it was real. As real as the woman of flash and fire here with him in his bed.

He knew, by the frantic way she clawed at the silken, chocolate-colored comforter beneath her, by the way she twisted and arched, moaning in pleasure, that he had brought Zooey to more than one climax. He'd used everything at his disposal—his tongue, his lips, his fingers—doing things with her that he'd never attempted with Patricia.

Yet here, with Zooey, it seemed right.

And then, because each time she lifted her hips, grasping for him, he wanted nothing more than to be with her on this journey, he found he couldn't hold back any longer. He'd stretched his endurance, his control, until it was a long, thin thread, threatening to snap.

Moving her legs apart with his knee, while her eyes held him prisoner, Jack drove himself into her. Passion and desire slammed into him with the force of a hydrogen bomb. As she began to move, to moan his name against his mouth, Jack realized he was twice as lost within her as he'd been before.

The journey to fulfillment was quick, euphoric, and he found himself wanting both the sensation and the anticipation of that sensation to exist at the same time. Wanting it to continue forever, or as much of forever as he could manage to hang on to.

Because he knew that logic and remorse waited for him just around the corner. More than anything, he wanted to elude both for as long as humanly possible.

Longer.

So after the last glorious sensation had shuddered through him, Jack gathered Zooey to him on the bed and held her for a very long time. Losing himself in the scent of her body, the silky way her hair felt against his skin.

So this was paradise.

This was what perfect felt like, Zooey

thought, a sweet, dreamy sensation swirling through her as she curled her body into his.

Jack wasn't her first lover, but, she realized, he was her first love.

She'd been engaged to Connor, coming together with him because at the time it seemed as if it was the thing to do. It was what everyone else wanted from her. She'd remained engaged to Connor, even though something inside of her had resisted, because she knew it would make her parents happy. Connor had not been without appeal. But you could only take a relationship so far because of a sense of responsibility. After that, it began to fall apart if its foundations weren't based on anything solid. Anything real.

Tonight was real. Very real. As were her feelings for Jack.

She didn't want to leave. Not his bedroom, not the moment. She knew that for the rest of her life, she was going to be trying to recapture this sensation. And the promise of finding it, of having it again, no matter how briefly, was what was going to sustain her.

But even now, Zooey could feel Jack withdrawing. Pulling away from her. He wasn't actually moving aside, but she could feel his body tightening. As if he was physically attempting to reconstruct the barriers that had disintegrated tonight. The barriers that normally stood between them.

Too late, she crowed silently. You couldn't unring a bell, and hers had been rung. Over and over again. What had happened between them *had* happened. And every wonderful, delicious, unexpected moment was forever sealed in her memory.

Raising her head, Zooey looked at the man who was the father of the children she adored. An enigmatic smile played on her lips. She had no idea how that aroused him.

"So," she began, tracing her fingertip along his chest, "about the Christmas party…"

How could she talk about parties, about anything, after what they'd just done? After what they'd just shared? "You're kidding."

"Am I?"

There was mischief in her eyes, and even though he knew he should be getting up, should somehow be trying to rummage through the ashes to find the bits and pieces of his life the way it had been only an hour ago, he couldn't help being drawn to her again. Wanting her again.

Zooey was strumming her fingers down his chest, stroking it lightly with the familiarity of a longtime lover, not someone who had only breached the wall a scant few minutes ago.

He felt as if their souls had been together forever, even as he told himself he was being insane.

Zooey gave him the benefit of her thoughts. There really was logic behind her teasing question. "Parties seem to bring out the best in you." It certainly had tonight. "Or maybe it's the costume." Her eyes crinkled as she grinned. "How do you feel about putting on a Santa Claus suit?"

Jack grabbed her hand to keep her from distracting him, and held on to it as he talked.

"Oh, no," he declared firmly. "This time, I mean it," he added, in case she was actually serious. With Zooey, he had no clue, no way to second-guess her. Had she been on a jury he was pleading a case before, he would have been entirely uncertain how the verdict might go.

She was unpredictable. He was the predictable one. Or at least, he would have said he was—until tonight. Until she'd taken his hand, led him to the stairs and managed to send him over the brink, into a land he had no previous knowledge of. He had nothing to help guide him. Nothing to light his way as he tried to navigate to a safe harbor.

Being with Zooey didn't make him feel safe. Didn't make him feel complacent. But he discovered that for the first time in his life, being safe wasn't all that important to him.

Because of Zooey, inspired by Zooey, he found himself wanting to be reckless, daring.

Wanting, he realized, to make love to her again. Because while he was making love with her, he didn't have to think. All that was required of him was to react. And he could do that. With her.

He gave her an alternative to her plan, just in case she was seriously entertaining the idea he was fairly certain she'd tossed out on a lark. "You can be Mrs. Claus, or one of the elves."

She wasn't ready to give up her suggestion. "You'd look cute dressed up as Santa." And then the gleam in her eye became positively wicked. "But I have to admit, you look even cuter not dressed at all."

Grasping her hips, he drew her over him until she was on top. "Funny, I was thinking the very same thing."

Her hair rained down around his face like golden sunbeams. "What else were you thinking?"

He could feel himself hardening again. Wanting her. "Guess."

Zooey shifted ever so slightly, just enough to arouse him further. "I don't think I have to. I think I might have a clue," she told him, right before she brought her mouth down to his.

Chapter Fourteen

"Morning!"

Zooey sang out the greeting cheerfully when Jack finally walked into the kitchen the following morning. She was surprised he'd taken so long to come down. Even the children were up and ready and at the table before him.

Maybe last night had worn him out, she thought with a smile. He'd been sleeping when she'd slipped out of his room, taking the precaution just in case Emily or Jackie woke up and went looking for either her or Jack. She'd been tempted just to lie there, watching him sleep, but sense won over temptation. This time.

Zooey turned down the flame beneath the frying pan and the newest batch of French toast. She felt remarkably cheerful for a woman who had slept a total of six and a half, maybe seven, minutes the entire night. But she was still flying high on adrenaline and a double dose of euphoria.

Last night had been like a dream come true. Jack had been everything she'd always thought a lover should be. Tender, kind and completely involved in ensuring her pleasure above his own. Given that, along with the fact that he was handsome and successful, she had no idea why this man didn't have droves of women following him wherever he went.

Whatever the reason, she was glad he didn't, because she hated having to worry about how she measured up against another woman.

As of this moment, she thought, watching Jack come in, life was absolutely perfect.

She saw his eyes dart in her general direction. Jack barely nodded his head. Something that sounded like "Morning," emerged from his lips, but it could have just been that he was clearing his throat. He also only vaguely acknowledged the children at the table, only after Emily said something to him twice, repeating it when he didn't respond to her the first time.

Taking the mug of extra black coffee she'd poured a second ago, Zooey placed it in Jack's free hand. With a smile, she stepped back and indicated the French toast that was still in the frying pan.

"I made breakfast."

She noticed that he didn't release his hold on his briefcase.

"I don't have time." He didn't even look at her as he said it. His attention seemed to be riveted to the back door. And escape.

Maybe not so perfect, Zooey silently amended. But then, just because the earth had moved for her last night didn't necessarily mean that it had for him, even though, until just this moment, she would have sworn on a stack of Bibles that Jack had been as swept away by what had happened last night as she was.

"Breakfast is the most important meal of the day, Daddy," Emily informed him. Her tone of voice indicated that she felt she was imparting important information that could also be classified as breaking news. As a clincher, she added, "My teacher says so."

"And she's right," Zooey agreed. She kept

one eye on Jack, who was frowning. She didn't want him to feel as if she was trying to be pushy, or at least pushier than she'd been. The last thing she wanted was for him to think that she felt last night gave her special privileges, such as the right to tell him what to do. "But sometimes, people don't have time to eat breakfast at the table. They eat it on the run."

Anticipating that he might be in a hurry because it was Monday and because he was Jack, she'd wrapped up a serving of French toast, complete with syrup in a small, airtight container, and packed it to go.

"Here." Smiling, Zooey handed him the bag she'd prepared. "Run."

Jackie's eyes lit up. "Run, Daddy, run!" he exclaimed excitedly, waving his feet back and forth for added momentum.

Draining the last of the coffee, Jack put the mug down and looked down at the bag she'd put in his hand. "What's this?"

"Breakfast," she told him simply. Since he hadn't been down here first thing in the morning as usual, she was pretty sure he'd overslept. Which made him late. "I had a feeling you might be in a hurry this morning."

He was. But he was fairly sure it wasn't the way she thought.

He was in a hurry to get away from the feelings that had insisted on rising up and haunting him in his dreams all night, no matter how hard he tried to ignore them or banish them.

Feelings that he felt entirely unequal to dealing with. He had no idea what to make of them or how to react.

All he knew was that he felt as if he was coming unraveled. And he didn't like it.

"Yeah," he mumbled. "Thanks." Without any further communication, either to his children or to her, he made his way out the back door to the garage.

"See you tonight," she called after him just as he was about to shut the door.

He paused only long enough to give her fair warning. "I might be late."

The way Jack said it, she had a feeling he was planning on it.

And she was right.

Jack didn't come home. Not at the usual time, or the time he often walked through the door when he was late. By eleven, Zooey gave up waiting. She turned off the warming tray with his dinner in the kitchen and went upstairs to bed. Despite her disappointment at

his no-show, she was still desperately clinging to the shred of euphoria that continued to
hover around her, telling herself that this was
business as usual for Jack. At this point, she
should have been more than used to it.

Except it wasn't supposed to be business
as usual, she argued with herself as she lay in
the bed a few minutes later, watching shad-
ows on the wall. Some part of Jack should
have been affected by what had happened
last night, shouldn't it?

Okay, she didn't exactly expect him to start
grinning from ear to ear and singing silly love
songs, but she also didn't expect him to au-
dition to play the phantom of Danbury Way.

The last thing she remembered thinking
before she fell asleep was that tomorrow
would be better.

But it wasn't. It was more of the same. If
anything, Jack became even more of a non-
entity than he had been before.

As each day went by, it progressively became worse. Instead of just working long
hours, he seemed to be working around the
clock, gone before Zooey got up in the morning, back after she'd gone to bed. It got to the
point that if it hadn't been for the wet towels

in his bathroom and the dishes that magically appeared in the sink, testifying that he had come home, showered and had something to eat before making good on another escape, she would have thought she'd made him up.

The second day he was gone, Jack left a voice message on the phone, telling her that he was involved in preparing a high profile case for trial, one that required all of his attention.

She knew in her heart it was more than that. There might have been a case, all right, but that wasn't making him turn into the invisible man. It was her.

Zooey thought of waiting up for him, of confronting him when he came home and making him own up to what was going on. And then make him explain to her why he was doing this. But while she felt perfectly justified in cornering him when it had something to do with the children's welfare, because this merely involved her—*them*—she couldn't get herself to do it. Because she shouldn't *have* to do it, she thought, fighting back tears. After one night of lovemaking with her, Jack Lever shouldn't suddenly have turned into Upstate New York's version of a hermit.

Had her techniques been that bad? she demanded silently in the privacy of her own room late at night. Had the idea of the two of them being intimate for any given length of time appalled him that much?

She had no answers.

All she had was a heart that was aching more and more. She couldn't make herself shrug this off, couldn't find a way to just lie low and wait it out. It hurt too much to be living in the same house, knowing that Jack was avoiding her like the plague.

And because of that, avoiding his children as well. That hurt just as much as his sudden abandonment of her.

"Is Daddy gone away on a trip?" Emily asked Friday morning as she and Olivia were being driven to school.

"Yes," Zooey answered quickly.

It was easier saying that than explaining to the girl that something had happened to make her father stay away. More than likely, Emily would want details.

"Is he going to be back soon?"

Zooey could tell by her tone of voice that the little girl sorely missed her father.

This had to stop, Zooey vowed. Before he

completely destroyed whatever relationship he had left with his children.

"Soon," she promised Emily.

Zooey knew of only one way to end Jack's self-imposed exodus and get him to start keeping regular hours at home again. It was a drastic step, but she had no choice other than to take it. Not if she wanted to keep her conscience clear. There was something far greater at stake here than her supposed love life.

Frances Finnegan sat very quietly at her desk. She tended to do that when she was in shock. Finally, she raised her eyes to her firstborn and formed the question she wished she didn't have to ask. Not when it followed a request that not only made her heart glad, but would make both her husband and her brother-in-law extremely happy.

"Zooey, are you sure?"

Zooey hadn't allowed herself to think. Once she'd decided on this course of action, she hadn't looked back, hadn't left herself the option to reconsider. She tried to sound as positive as she could as she replied, "Yes, I'm sure."

Frances wasn't buying it. She knew her

daughter too well, even if Zooey didn't think so. Though it wasn't really necessary, she took her for a trip down memory lane.

"But you said you didn't want to work here," she reminded her. "You even left college a month before graduation because you said you didn't fit into the business world." Frances gestured around the office. "And this is the business world, Zooey. Make no mistake about that."

Not wanting to go into her reasons for this sudden change, Zooey zeroed in on something minor her mother had said. "If you need me to have a degree to work here, I can complete the classes—"

Frances waved her hand dismissively. She was too savvy to allow herself to be snowed. "That's not my point, Zooey. My point was that you were adamant you didn't want to go into the family business."

Rather than sit on the chair in front of her mother's desk, or on the leather sofa off to one side, Zooey prowled around the room restlessly. She shrugged off her mother's words. "I was young."

Frances laughed. "You were a little more than a year younger than you are now."

Zooey paused to take a deep breath. She

shoved her hands into the pockets of her jeans. The emptiness that haunted her, that in part prompted her to do this, refused to go away. "A year is a long time."

Frances rose to her feet and rounded her desk until she was standing in front of her daughter. "Zooey, what happened?"

Zooey pressed her lips together, willing herself to sound cheerful, or at least not upset. "Nothing. I just grew up."

Her mom placed her hands on her shoulders, holding her still. Frances wanted to hug her, to hold her the way she had when Zooey was little and she could make her problems go away with a few comforting words, accompanied by a bowl of strawberry ice cream. But she knew Zooey was in a fragile place right now. Hugging would not be welcomed. It would be confused with pity. "That's not what I'm seeing in your eyes."

Zooey flashed a grin. "You always did let those eye doctor appointments slip by," she said fondly. Very gently, she separated herself from her mother's hold. "Really, Mom, I'm okay." And then, because she knew her mother could read her like a book, she added, "This is just for the best, that's all."

Whose best? Frances wondered. It certainly

didn't seem as if it was Zooey's. "What about those children you were taking care of?" she pressed. "Emily and Jackie. It seemed to me they were very attached to you."

Leaving them would be one of the hardest things she'd ever done, if not the hardest. But she had to go, for their own good. Because who knew how long Jack would avoid staying home if she was there?

So she shrugged carelessly and murmured, "They're young. They'll get attached to someone else." *Far easier than I will.*

As if she could read her mind, her mother asked, "Do you want them to?"

Zooey wasn't up to discussing this right now. The last thing she wanted was to let her mother see her cry. "Mom, this is a very simple question. Do you have a place for me or not?"

Frances slipped an arm around her shoulders. She couldn't remember them ever feeling this stiff. She pretended not to notice, but found herself wanting to box Jack Lever's ears even if she didn't know the man. Because he had to be at the bottom of this. Zooey was too crazy about those kids to want to leave on her own.

"Zooey, there's always a place for you here,

you know that. Your father'll be overjoyed when I tell him. So will your uncle. And what I feel about you coming back goes without saying, but—"

Zooey turned and looked at her, stopping her mother before anything further could be said. "All right, then it's settled."

Frances studied her firstborn for a long moment. There was no reasoning with her now. But then, that was nothing new. "If you say so, Zooey."

"You're leaving?"

The sparsely written note that she had slipped under his door in the middle of the night and that he had just discovered a minute ago on his way out, was crumpled in his hand as Jack burst into the kitchen the following Monday morning.

Zooey looked up from the scrambled eggs and ham she was making for the children. Jackie was in his high chair, making confetti out of his toast, while Emily sat primly at the table, nibbling on hers. Both children looked surprised to see their father.

"Yes," Zooey replied quietly, taking a spatula and dividing the contents of the pan between two plates. She hadn't bothered to make three portions. She had no appetite, and she hadn't been sure if she would even see Jack.

Emily looked stunned, then upset. "No!" she cried, staring at her.

"No!" Jackie echoed, without the slightest clue why his sister had uttered the word.

Damn it, she wasn't going to cry. Zooey tried to keep herself together as best as she could. "It's time, sweetheart," she told Emily.

"Why? Why is it time?" the child demanded, tears springing to her eyes. Trapping Zooey's soul there. "You can't go. You can't leave us." Zooey had just enough time to put down the pan before Emily flung herself at her, wrapping her arms around her waist and holding on tight. "You can't! I won't let you go."

This was ripping her apart, Zooey thought. Very gently, she removed Emily's arms and then stooped down to the little girl's level. It took everything she had not to drag her into her arms and hold her tightly. But it was reason that was needed right now, not emotion.

Zooey was painfully aware that Jack wasn't saying anything, which just proved to her that this was ultimately the right course to take.

She kept her eyes on Emily. "Just because

I won't be living here anymore doesn't mean that I'm leaving you or your brother. I'll always be around if you need me," she promised, her voice low, husky, as she struggled to keep it from breaking.

Reaching into her pocket, Zooey took out a business card with the company logo embossed on it. It had the address of Finnegan's Fine Furniture's corporate offices. She'd written her cell phone number, too, in preparation for this moment.

Nothing could have prepared her, though, she realized, her heart feeling like lead in her chest.

She placed the card in Emily's hand and closed her fingers over it. "All you have to do is call this number and I'll come."

Emily grasped the card. Tears began to spill down her cheeks. "It's not the same," she whispered.

"No," Zooey agreed. "It's not the same. But it's almost the same. It's close. Just like I'll be." She pointed to the address on the card. "This isn't really all that far away."

"It's farther than your room," Emily sobbed.

"It is," Zooey agreed heavily.

Jack had not said anything at all beyond the first initial expression of surprise. He was still standing there, looking at her, not even trying to alleviate his daughter's distress.

She was right, Zooey thought, feeling lost. Feeling alone. He wanted her to leave. Wanted her to leave so much that he wasn't even willing to offer up a token protest to make Emily feel better.

How could she have been so wrong about someone? Zooey wondered.

Served her right for dreaming. For hoping. There was no such thing as perfect men, no such thing as perfect moments. If ever she'd had any doubts, Jack had just shown her that there weren't.

Jack remained walled in his silence, not trusting his voice, not trusting his emotions.

He didn't want Zooey to leave. More than anything, he didn't want her to go. But he'd known in his gut that this was coming. Known as surely as the sun would rise that this had to be the natural consequence of what had happened between them Halloween night. He should have found a way to maintain control.

Too late. Damage done.

He couldn't blame her. Only himself. The situation had turned awkward between them almost instantly. He'd certainly felt it. Because that one night had not satisfied him, it had just shown him what had been missing from his life. Had shown him that he wanted more. And all of this had placed Zooey in a terrible dilemma. Her "employer" had made love with her and he wanted to do it again. If she gave in, would she do so because she didn't want to lose her job? Because she didn't want to leave the children? Or because she had feelings for him?

Jack was certain that the last, if it factored in at all, came a very distant third. So, as much as he wanted her, he'd been trying to give Zooey as much space as was humanly possible. To make her feel that he wasn't going to crowd her, wasn't going to demand repeat performances of the other night if she didn't want any to take place.

And still she was leaving. Because she was undoubtedly afraid that he would put more moves on her.

Her fear had to be tremendous, since he knew how much she loved his children. It was there in everything she did for them and with them. For her to leave them meant she just couldn't cope with the idea that things might heat up between them again. The fear that perhaps, some night, he might force himself on her.

He thought of telling her he'd never do that, but it would be a matter of protesting too much. It would only convince her that she was right in the first place.

So, as much as he wanted to tear up the note she'd left for him, refuse to accept her resignation and to have her remain here permanently, his hands were tied. He couldn't impose his will on her.

The best thing he could do for Zooey would be to let her go. Even though doing it twisted a knife in his gut.

"How soon?" he finally asked, his voice devoid of all emotion.

God, he couldn't wait to get rid of her, could he? Zooey thought, fighting back tears. Well, if he didn't care, she wasn't going to let him see that she did. She didn't want him thinking even less of her.

"As soon as you can line up someone to watch the children," she said in a voice that matched his own.

"Don't worry about that." There were temporary agencies he could turn to until he could find someone suitable. "I don't want to interfere with your plans." And then he paused, searching her face. Maybe this was a ruse for some reason. "You are going somewhere after this, aren't you?"

"Yes." She bit off the word wanting to use the frying pan behind her for more than just making eggs. She struggled to get hold of her temper. "Yes," she repeated more calmly, "I have something lined up."

"All right," he agreed, his voice calm, distant, "then I'll make the arrangements and you can be on your way by tomorrow."

Zooey felt as if her stomach had dropped out. He was all but giving her the bum's rush. Why? Was he that appalled at being involved with her?

"Perfect," she replied tersely.

"Perfect," he echoed.

He'd been hoping, even as he made the offer, that Zooey would change her mind at the last second. That she would tell him she needed more time. Stall. Give him some kind of sign, *any* kind of a sign, that maybe she wanted to stay. Stay with the children. Stay with him.

But since she was saying yes almost eagerly, he knew he'd just been deluding himself. She wanted to leave. Quickly.

Served him right for giving in to his impulses, for having the audacity to think that someone as bright, as outgoing as Zooey would want to be with someone as settled, as set in his ways, as he was.

"If you need references—" he began.

"I don't need references," she almost snapped. Zooey raised her chin. She kept one arm around Emily, wishing she could take the kids with her. Jack didn't deserve to have children. "I'm all set, actually."

He nodded, picking up his briefcase. "Then I guess there's really nothing more to be said on the subject."

"No," she agreed in the same tone, "nothing more."

Chapter Fifteen

Every day seemed that much worse than the one before.

Zooey didn't know how much more she could take. It was supposed to be getting better, not worse. She'd never felt like this before—like a drowning victim dragged back from the brink of death who couldn't seem to suck in enough air to make her feel as if survival was an actual option.

She couldn't shake it, couldn't seem to work her way past it. She just kept moving through the pea soup fog, waiting for it to clear up.

It didn't.

Because she'd taken all her things with her when she left Danbury Way, Zooey was figuratively among the homeless when she reported in for work at the corporate offices the first day. That was quickly remedied by her mother, who immediately threw open the door of her old room. To make the invitation to take up residence in the house where she'd been born more appealing and less off-putting, Frances, clever soul that she was, had told her she was welcome to stay there until she found something more to her liking.

The trouble was, Zooey thought as she prowled around her office, restless and exhausted at the same time, she wasn't out looking. There seemed to be no energy in her veins to prompt her to go from apartment to apartment, looking for someplace to make her own. She of the boundless energy suddenly had barely enough to get out of bed and dressed in the morning.

Zooey told herself that she was coming down with something. "Something" kept coming for an entire two weeks without ever taking shape, hovering in the background. Making itself known just enough so that she felt as if each limb weighed a thousand pounds and could be moved only with the greatest of effort.

One day loosely worked into another. Like a prisoner sentenced to life without parole, she lost track of time.

Days no longer meant anything to her. They were just something to get through, nothing more.

"Not that I don't love having you around, Zooey, but I just don't know what to do with you."

Frances Finnegan looked at her daughter over the tops of the glasses nature and her ophthalmologist had forced her to wear in order to read words smaller than a billboard. She'd summoned Zooey into her office this morning after reviewing the halfhearted report that had come from her daughter's computer concerning the next six months' sales projections. It was obvious that not only was Zooey's heart not in it, her mind appeared to be AWOL as well.

Thinking that it was time to shake her up and have a serious heart-to-heart, Frances said as much to her daughter.

"This report was written by someone whose mind kept wandering away from its subject." Even her brother-in-law, who was awful when it came to report writing, could do a better job than what she had lying on her desk. This just wasn't her Zooey, and Frances meant to find out why.

A rueful expression passed over Zooey's face. Reaching for the report, she took it from her mother's desk. "I'll do better."

"You'd have to work hard at doing worse," Frances said honestly, then sighed. "Zooey, I'm trying to figure out what you are doing here. Your coming to work for the family business is certainly not working out."

Zooey raised her chin defensively, a spark of her old self returning, much to her mom's relief. "I need a period of adjustment."

But Frances shook her head. She'd never expected to hear herself say this. "You need to go back to where you came from."

Zooey's eyes widened. She hadn't envisioned this. "Are you firing me?"

"I'm freeing you," Frances corrected.

She didn't want to be freed, Zooey thought, a slight edge of panic slicing through her. She *needed* to work, not so much for the money but because it gave her someplace to be, something to do, however badly. If she just sat at home, she'd lose what little mind she still had.

"Mom, I'm sorry, I'll do better," Zooey promised.

She saw the look in her mother's eyes. The same look that had been there when she was growing up. The look that said the truth was required from her. So the truth came. Or at least the part she could put into words.

"It's just that... I keep wondering if they're okay. Emily and Jackie," she added, realizing she was verbally jumping around.

There was more to it than that and they both knew it, but for now, Frances played along. "If that's all that's on your mind, why don't you just call them and find out?"

"I don't want to—" Zooey stopped herself. She'd almost said that she didn't want to take a chance on having Jack pick up the phone, but that was something she didn't want to share yet. Maybe never. "Interfere," she finally said. "I don't want to interfere," she repeated. "They're adjusting to a new nanny. Having me call and talk to them will just set them back to square one."

An almost amused expression played on her mother's lips. "Maybe they're not adjusting to the new nanny. Maybe they hate her."

Zooey looked at her for a long, poignant moment, as if that thought hadn't crossed her mind a hundred times already. "You know,

I never realized how much you and I think alike."

Frances laughed. "Your best qualities come from me, Zooey. The other ones, blame your father." And then she grew serious. "Zooey, you're going to have to move on or move back." It wasn't anything that Zooey hadn't told herself more than once since she'd walked out of Jack's house. "This wavering in the middle—"

"Move on," Zooey declared fiercely, in case her mother had any doubts. "I want to move on. It's just taking me longer than I thought, that's all." Crossing to her mother's desk, she perched on one corner, feeling helpless. She'd never been in this kind of position before and didn't know how to get out of it. "The moment I decided to put Connor behind me, he was history. So was college and every job I ever had."

"Except for this last one."

"Except for this last one," Zooey echoed. She looked down at her mother. "I just need you to be patient with me, Mom."

"I have infinite patience." And it was true. She'd proved it more than once while Zooey was growing up. But there was a time to cut her daughter some slack and a time to tighten the reins. "The business, however, would like you to get up to speed a little faster than you've been doing. A lot faster, actually," she amended. "Quarterly reports are just around the corner—"

Zooey nodded vigorously. "I know, I know." She slid off the desk. "I promise I'll do better."

"Good." Frances rose to her feet as well. She slipped an arm around her daughter's shoulders, walking her to the door. "You'll make your father very happy—if that's what you want."

What I want isn't going to happen, Zooey thought.

She did her best not to make the smile she forced to her lips look as if it was merely painted on. "Always like to see you and Dad happy."

Frances gave her a penetrating look. "You know what I mean."

"Yes, I know what you mean." Before leaving, Zooey paused to kiss her mother's cheek. She'd never really appreciated her before, she thought. "Thanks, Mom."

She was aware that her mother continued watching her as she walked down the hall.

Moving at a quicker pace than she had for the last two weeks, Zooey started back to the office she'd been given, silently vowing to do better. She owed it to her mom, if not both her parents.

As she hurried past the receptionist, the woman half rose in her chair. "I put them in your office."

Confused, Zooey looked at her. As far as she knew, nothing was being delivered to her. "Put what into my office?"

"The kids. I didn't think you wanted me to interrupt you when you were in with Mrs. Finnegan, and I didn't know what to do with them—"

The last part of her statement was addressed to Zooey's back.

Zooey flew the rest of the way to her office. She didn't need to ask "What kids?" She knew. Emily and Jackie. Alone?

Her heart lodged itself in her throat as half a dozen scenarios, none of them good, flashed through her mind like a doomsday kaleidoscope.

The second Zooey opened the door, Emily and Jackie rushed toward her. She dropped to her knees just in time to have the children fling themselves at her, surrounding her with small arms and huge doses of affection.

"We missed you, Zooey," Emily cried, hugging her as hard as she could.

"Missed you!" Jackie echoed, the words thundering into her left ear.

"And I missed you." Zooey kissed them both more than once and held them to her tightly for a long moment before finally releasing them. She drew back to look at their faces. She needed answers. Lots of answers. "What are you doing here?"

Emily's lower lip quivered, as if she expected to be rejected and sent away. "You said to come if we needed you."

"No," Zooey corrected gently, "I said to call and *I'd* come if you needed me." This had *desperate* written all over it, she thought.

Rising, she took each child by the hand and led them over to the love seat against the wall. It was just large enough for the three of them.

Zooey sat down with a child on either side. To her surprise, instead of squirming, Jackie curled up beside her and laid his head in her lap. She'd never seen him so docile before. She stroked his hair as she posed questions to Emily.

"How did you get here? Did your dad bring you?"

"No." Emily looked up at her with big, innocent eyes. "We took a taxi."

Zooey stared at the little girl, stunned. "A taxi?" Taxis here didn't roam the streets the way they did in the city.

Emily nodded. "Olivia helped me find one in the telephone book and we called it together. I showed the man the address on the card you gave me."

"How did you pay for it?" Was there a driver outside, waiting for his money and getting progressively angrier?

"I used the money in my piggy bank," Emily told her. "And he brought us here."

This wasn't right. A seven-year-old and an almost-three-year-old weren't supposed to be out, wandering around alone like that. Why didn't the cab driver ask about adult supervision? "Where's your nanny?"

"Sleeping." Emily leaned closer and confided, "She sleeps a lot. The yellow medicine from the bottle she keeps in her pocket makes her sleep when she takes it."

Damn it, what kind of people was Jack leaving his kids with? Why didn't he do a thorough check into the woman's references before he hired her? "Did you tell your daddy that she sleeps so much?"

Emily shook her head. "Daddy's so sad, I didn't want to make him sadder." The little girl looked up at her. "I saw him looking at your picture."

Emily was making this up. Zooey had never given Jack a photograph of herself. "Your daddy doesn't have a picture of me, Emily."

"Yes, he does," she insisted. "It's the one that Olivia's mommy took at the Halloween party. Daddy was in it, too."

As soon as Emily said it, Zooey remembered Angela aiming the camera at them and ordering, "Smile." Zooey recalled being surprised that Jack hadn't turned his head away at the last minute. Until that moment, she would have said that he wasn't the type to pose for photographs.

"Olivia's mommy came to the house last week to give it to him. Daddy looks sadder every time he looks at it. He has it on his desk." Emily wiggled up to her knees on the cushion, lowering her voice as she whispered into her ear. "He told me he misses you."

Emily's warm breath grazed her cheek even as her words grazed her heart. Zooey resisted believing the girl. Resisted because more than anything in the world, she wanted it to be true. She wanted Jack to have missed her half as much as she'd missed him these last two weeks.

But she knew that Emily was very bright, very creative for her age. It wasn't beyond her to fabricate the story to get what she wanted.

Tucking one arm around the girl's small waist, Zooey told her seriously, "Your nose grows when you fib, Emily."

Instead of feeling to see if her nose had gotten any larger, Emily looked like the personification of innocence as she insisted, "He misses you, Zooey."

Then why didn't the big jerk call?

Beginning to feel like her old self, Zooey made up her mind on the spur of the moment. Moving Jackie into an upright position, she rose to her feet.

"C'mon," she declared.

Emily instantly hopped off the love seat. "Where are we going?"

Not waiting for Jackie to clamber to his feet, she picked him up. Stopping only long enough to get her purse from her desk and to slip her poncho over her head, she reclaimed Emily's hand. "To see your dad and let him know where his children are."

Zooey hurried past the receptionist again.

The woman looked on in confusion. "Where are you going, Ms. Finnegan?"

Possibly to hell, Zooey thought. "I need to tell Jack Lever that he picked a lousy nanny to watch his kids."

There was a meeting scheduled for four o'clock. A meeting that the woman knew Zooey was supposed to be attending. "You can't—" the receptionist began, rounding her desk to try to catch up to the threesome.

"Oh, yes, I can," Zooey retorted as she turned the corner toward the elevators.

For the first time in more than two weeks, Zooey felt like smiling.

The inner-sanctum quiet of the law firm of Wasserman, Kendall, Lake & Lever was shattered the moment the elevator doors parted. Office doors all along the corridor were opened by occupants curious to see what the commotion was all about. It sounded as if a busload of children had been deposited there.

Not bothering to attempt to get Jackie to lower his voice, Zooey slowed down only when she reached Jack's office.

Lost in thought, a state aided and abetted by a malaise that threatened to completely undo him, Jack rose from his desk and opened the door when the vaguely familiar noise sounded as if it was growing louder.

His face almost came in contact with Zooey's fist.

He would have been less stunned to see Noah saying he was there to collect two of everything. "Zooey."

About to knock, she dropped her hand. She set Jackie down inside the threshold, then took his hand as well as Emily's and held them up.

"Missing something?" she asked Jack.

The sarcastic question had a simple enough answer. Or so she thought. The answer she received wasn't the one she was expecting.

"Yes," he told her quietly, finally finding his tongue. "You."

With the wind suddenly sucked out of her sails, Zooey was left completely stunned. Positive that her mind had put words into his mouth, she hoarsely asked, "What?"

Aware that everyone on the floor had suddenly volunteered to become unofficial witnesses to his every word, Jack drew Zooey and his children into his office and shut the door behind him.

Because it was his nature to be orderly, he

backtracked. There were blanks that needed filling in. "What are you doing here?"

Now that sounded more like Jack, she thought. The other had been a momentary out-of-body experience. There couldn't be any other explanation for what she thought she'd heard.

"Showing you that while you might be a great lawyer, you're lousy when it comes to finding a nanny for your own children." It was very hard trying to remain angry with him when everything inside of her ached to be with him again.

Where was her pride? she demanded silently.

Since his mind had been focused on her all this time, it was only natural that he thought she was referring to herself, not the lackluster woman in the sensible shoes he'd taken on to fill the vacancy Zooey's departure had left. He couldn't bring himself to think of the woman as taking Zooey's place because there was no way she could manage to do that. Zooey was an impossible act to follow, on all counts.

"Oh, I don't know—"

Zooey didn't let him get any further. She wasn't about to get snowed by lawyer rhetoric.

"Well, I do. Emily and Jackie came to my office. In a cab," she stressed heatedly. "Emily told me the nanny was asleep, something she apparently does with a fair amount of regularity after drinking." Zooey's eyes were blazing now as she came at him. "Don't you check references?"

God, but he wanted to kiss her. For the first time in more than two weeks, he felt alive. It took effort to hold himself in check. To not at least touch her face. "She was just a temp."

That was a lousy excuse and he knew it, Zooey thought. "And the damage she could have done to the kids might have been permanent." She blew out a breath. Her exasperation mounted. "You obviously need help."

He couldn't take his eyes off her. Part of him was afraid that if he did, she would vanish like a dream and this had to be a dream, because both of his children were here—and quiet, something he knew was a complete impossibility.

"Yes," he agreed, keeping a straight face, "I do."

She made another impulsive decision. One

she'd been longing to execute ever since she'd walked out of his house. "Okay, I'll come back to work until you can find a new nanny."

Jack summoned his best poker face. "That might be hard."

Wasn't he going to allow her to come back? Was he that angry at her for quitting? "Why?"

The corners of his mouth rose just the slightest bit. Or maybe that was her imagination again. "Because I won't be looking for a new one."

Did he want her to handle that, too? Didn't he see how necessary it was to get involved in his children's lives? Selecting the right nanny was crucial to their development, not to mention their happiness. He had to be made to understand that.

"I know you're busy, Jack, but these are your kids we're talking about."

He took a deep breath before answering. Not to fortify himself, but to fill his head with the scent of her shampoo. He'd never realized he was so partial to jasmine until she was no longer there.

"I know. But the kids don't want a nanny," he informed her. "They want you."

Damn, but he was making her feel awful.

Zooey shook her head. "That's not going to work out," she told him solemnly.

"Why?" he asked. "Why won't it work out?" Because he intended to make it work out, no matter what it took.

She told him the truth. "Because I can't work for a man who's not there."

And the way she saw it, since he hadn't tried to get in contact with her, it meant he was glad she was gone, no matter what Emily said to the contrary. And if he was relieved to have her gone, he'd revert to playing those awful games of hide and seek again if she did come back. Forget that it hurt her; it was awful for the children.

He nodded, his expression indicating that he thought her protest was reasonable. "What if I promise to be there more often?"

She wasn't about to get captured by a lawyer's rhetoric. "How often?"

Suppressing a grin, he lobbed the ball back into her court. "How often would you like?"

She thought a moment. He was coming across as extremely accommodating. Maybe she'd misjudged him. Maybe he was partial to his children, after all.

"Normal hours would be nice. To see you in the morning and at some reasonable hour at night so that Emily and Jackie don't forget what you look like."

"Done."

There hadn't even been a moment's hesitation. She couldn't help being suspicious. "Just like that?"

"Just like that," he assured her. "Whatever it takes to get you back into our—into my life," he amended.

Jack watched as surprise washed over her face. He knew that if he wanted her, he was going to have to be willing to step up to the plate, to say what she wanted to hear. What had resided silently in his heart up to now.

He needed to tell her what he felt, not what he thought sounded right.

"Your life," Zooey repeated, certain that she had to be hearing things.

As his children watched, Jack took her hand in his. "My life."

"You need a nanny, too?" She thought that might amuse the children, but this time, she didn't hear Emily giggling. Instead, she could have sworn she heard the little girl suck in her breath and then hold it in what seemed like anticipation.

"I don't know about a nanny," Jack replied, "but I need you."

Maybe she was hallucinating. "You need me," she repeated, mystified.

His eyes never left hers. "Yes."

She was going to need clarification. To have everything spelled out before she was going to allow her imagination to run away with her.

"For what?"

"To make the sun come up in the morning. To make my day."

It was her turn to look amused. "Like Clint Eastwood?"

Jack was still holding her hand, afraid that if he released it, she'd walk out on him again.

"You're a hell of a lot prettier than Clint Eastwood." He took a breath, then plunged in. "The kids need a mother. I need a wife…"

Her heart slammed against her chest. She had no idea how she managed to even frame a sentence. "You make it sound like a want ad."

"The key word is *want*," he told her. "The kids want you back, and God knows I do. I love you, Zooey. I've been thinking of nothing else since you left."

She was afraid to let herself believe that. Afraid of getting hurt again.

"You knew where to find me. It wasn't exactly a secret. Emily had the card with the address on it," she reminded him.

"I didn't want to make you do anything you didn't want to do." And in putting what he thought were her wishes ahead of his own, he'd wasted valuable time. Because it didn't look as if those had been her wishes at all.

She laughed softly to herself. "A noble lawyer. What a concept."

"Yes," he agreed, slipping his arms around her. To his relief, she didn't back away. God, but it felt good to hold her again. "But nobility only goes so far. When I saw you just now, with the kids, I decided I didn't want to be noble anymore."

A smile played along her lips. "What do you want to be?"

"Married." And then, in case he wasn't making himself clear, he said, "Zooey, will you marry us?"

Zooey could feel tears forming. "I always did love package deals."

"Then it's yes?" Emily cried.

Zooey spared her a glance. "Absolutely."

"You're supposed to kiss Daddy now," Emily told her, "so it's official."

Zooey laughed. "How do you know that?"

"I watch TV," the little girl replied with an air of one who wasn't to be argued with.

"Kiss Daddy," Jackie echoed.

"Not a hardship," Zooey murmured as she wrapped her arms around Jack's neck, whispered, "I love you, too," and did as the children had instructed.

* * * * *

HOMETOWN HEARTS ♥

YES! Please send me **The Hometown Hearts Collection** in Larger Print. This collection begins with 3 FREE books and 2 FREE gifts in the first shipment. Along with my 3 free books, I'll also get the next 4 books from the Hometown Hearts Collection, in LARGER PRINT, which I may either return and owe nothing, or keep for the low price of $4.99 U.S./ $5.89 CDN each plus $2.99 for shipping and handling per shipment*. If I decide to continue, about once a month for 8 months I will get 6 or 7 more books, but will only need to pay for 4. That means 2 or 3 books in every shipment will be FREE! If I decide to keep the entire collection, I'll have paid for only 32 books because 19 books are FREE! I understand that accepting the 3 free books and gifts places me under no obligation to buy anything. I can always return a shipment and cancel at any time. My free books and gifts are mine to keep no matter what I decide.

262 HCN 3432 462 HCN 3432

Name _____ (PLEASE PRINT) _____

Address _____ Apt. # _____

City _____ State/Prov. _____ Zip/Postal Code _____

Signature (if under 18, a parent or guardian must sign)

Mail to the **Reader Service:**
IN U.S.A.: P.O. Box 1867, Buffalo, NY. 14240-1867
IN CANADA: P.O. Box 609, Fort Erie, Ontario L2A 5X3

* Terms and prices subject to change without notice. Prices do not include applicable taxes. Sales tax applicable in NY. Canadian residents will be charged applicable taxes. This offer is limited to one order per household. All orders subject to approval. Credit or debit balances in a customer's account(s) may be offset by any other outstanding balance owed by or to the customer. Please allow 4 to 6 weeks for delivery. Offer available while quantities last. Offer not available to Quebec residents.

Get 2 Free Books,

Plus 2 Free Gifts—

just for trying the Reader Service!

Get 2 Free Books,
Plus 2 Free Gifts—
just for trying the Reader Service!

HARLEQUIN *super romance*

YES! Please send me 2 FREE LARGER-PRINT Harlequin® Superromance® novels and my 2 FREE gifts (gifts are worth about $10 retail). After receiving them, if I don't wish to receive any more books, I can return the shipping statement marked "cancel." If I don't cancel, I will receive 4 brand-new novels every month and be billed just $6.19 per book in the U.S. or $6.49 per book in Canada. That's a savings of at least 11% off the cover price! It's quite a bargain! Shipping and handling is just 50¢ per book in the U.S. or 75¢ per book in Canada.* I understand that accepting the 2 free books and gifts places me under no obligation to buy anything. I can always return a shipment and cancel at any time. The free books and gifts are mine to keep no matter what I decide.

132/332 HDN GLWS

Name	(PLEASE PRINT)

Address	Apt. #

City	State/Prov.	Zip/Postal Code

Signature (if under 18, a parent or guardian must sign)

Mail to the **Reader Service:**
IN U.S.A.: P.O. Box 1341, Buffalo, NY 14240-8531
IN CANADA: P.O. Box 603, Fort Erie, Ontario L2A 5X3

Want to try two free books from another line?
Call 1-800-873-8635 today or visit www.ReaderService.com.

* Terms and prices subject to change without notice. Prices do not include applicable taxes. Sales tax applicable in N.Y. Canadian residents will be charged applicable taxes. Offer not valid in Quebec. This offer is limited to one order per household. Books received may not be as shown. Not valid for current subscribers to Harlequin Superromance Larger-Print books. All orders subject to approval. Credit or debit balances in a customer's account(s) may be offset by any other outstanding balance owed by or to the customer. Please allow 4 to 6 weeks for delivery. Offer available while quantities last.

Your Privacy—The Reader Service is committed to protecting your privacy. Our Privacy Policy is available online at www.ReaderService.com or upon request from the Reader Service.

We make a portion of our mailing list available to reputable third parties that offer products we believe may interest you. If you prefer that we not exchange your name with third parties, or if you wish to clarify or modify your communication preferences, please visit us at www.ReaderService.com/consumerschoice or write to us at Reader Service Preference Service, P.O. Box 9062, Buffalo, NY 14240-9062. Include your complete name and address.

HSRLP17R